BEHIND EVERY GOOD MAN . . .

"We lost money on this gig because of you, you lit-tle—" Wilkins shut up suddenly when Slocum stepped over the baron and faced the sharpshooter. Wilkins's rage didn't diminish when he saw Slocum.

"You. I might have known you were still with him." Wilkins let out a bull roar and attacked.

Slocum ducked under a poorly aimed punch, stepped for-ward, and drove his fist as hard as he could into Wilkins's belly. The man folded like a bad poker hand and dropped to his knees. Slocum never hesitated. He took a half-step back, wound up, and kicked, the tip of his boot connecting square-ly with Wilkins's chin. The sharpshooter tumbled to the side, unconscious. Then all hell broke loose around Slocum. He was shoved and pushed, and men tried to pummel him. He rode the storm of fighting men like a leaf floating on a turbulent river.

The report from a Winchester froze everyone. Maddy swung the rifle around, cocking it again. This time she lowered it and aimed into the crowd.

"Which of you is first to get a bullet in the gut?"

SPECIAL PREVIEW!

Turn to the back of this book for a sneak-peek excerpt of the new epic western series . . .

THE HORSEMEN

. . . the sprawling, unforgettable story of a family of horse breeders and trainers—from the Civil War South to the Wild West.

OTHER BOOKS BY JAKE LOGAN

JAKE LOGAN

SLOCUM AND THE SHARPSHOOTER

BERKLEY BOOKS, NEW YORK

SLOCUM AND THE SHARPSHOOTER

A Berkley Book / published by arrangement with
the author

PRINTING HISTORY
Berkley edition / June 1992

ISBN: 0-425-13303-6

A BERKLEY BOOK® TM 757,375
Berkley Books are published by The Berkley Publishing Group,
200 Madison Avenue, New York, New York 10016.
The name "BERKLEY" and the "B" logo
are trademarks belonging to Berkley Publishing Corporation.

PRINTED IN THE UNITED STATES OF AMERICA

10   9   8   7   6   5   4   3   2   1

1

John Slocum had been on the trail too long. He reined back his horse, hooked his leg around the saddle's worn pommel, and stared straight ahead. The name of the Utah town had been blasted smooth by wind and weather on the signpost a mile or two back, but any civilization, even deep in Mormon country, promised its share of hard liquor. The days he had spent on the trail had given him one dust storm of a thirst, but had not prepared him for what stood before him. Slocum rubbed the grit from his eyes and tried to believe what he saw walking not ten yards away.

"Step right up, friends," came the loud cry. "Don't be afraid of Jumbo! He's big, but he's gentle!"

The elephant trumpeted and reared back, balancing precariously on its hind legs. Slocum had to calm his horse when the elephant bellowed again, and he had to use his strong legs as well as the reins to keep the sorrel from bolting when the elephant stuck its trunk into a watering trough, drank a snoutful, and then sprayed it high into the air in a watery umbrella. The children in town who gathered to watch the spectacle were thrilled. Slocum wasn't. His mount had served him faithfully the past month, getting him away from a band of Ute raiders and a vengeful sheriff down in Durango. He didn't want the horse scared out of its wits by a strange beast. Horses, at the best of times, weren't bright animals, and Slocum had seen more than one bolt at its own shadow and damage itself severely.

"There, good sir, step down from your mount and try mine!" called the man carrying a long pole with a metal hook on the end. He poked under the elephant's trunk and twisted. The animal bellowed and clumsily dropped to its front knees. "Mount, sir, and ride through town like an East Indian maharajah!"

"Thank you kindly," Slocum said, still angry about the elephant spooking his horse. "Let one of them take a ride." Slocum motioned to the droves of children staring longingly at the elephant.

"Which will it be?" the elephant's handler cried. "I know. Jumbo's so big and strong, he can take you all!" One by one, a dozen children approached, some fearfully, but none turning and running from what might be the chance of a lifetime. When the full dozen were perched atop the elephant, the barker roared in delight, poked the elephant again, and got the ponderous beast moving along the street.

Slocum was happy to see it go. Dismounting and hitching his horse to a post, he shook some trail dust off, leaving a small brown drift at his feet. Kicking it aside, Slocum stepped up onto the boardwalk. Another loud cry caught his attention. His hand flashed to the Colt Navy in its cross-draw holster, but he paused. No revolver would bring down this magnificent beast. The tiger in its cage snarled and pawed at the air as its handler passed out broadsides. Although he backed away, Slocum found one pressed into his hand.

Sells Brothers Circus, it announced proudly in crisp, flowing printed script. Slocum leaned against a post and watched as the animals made their slow parade past him. He had to admire the variety of the animals. Some he had seen before in other places, but this circus had a few he couldn't identify. Slocum always suspected a fraud when he saw something out of the ordinary. This innate skepticism had kept him alive—with a few dollars jingling in his pockets—when others lost their fortunes and sometimes even their lives.

"What's that one?" he shouted at a trainer prodding an awkward bird fully matching Slocum's six-foot height. The long, scrawny neck had an Adam's apple the size of a large man's fist, and its pointed head bobbed up and down constantly.

"This is an ostrich from the dark and forbidden continent of Africa!" came the immediate answer. "It lays eggs the size of your head! Come to the Sells Brothers Circus performance this evening and see for yourself!"

With that, the trainer hurried after the bird, which had strutted off with its peculiar gait in a direction perpendicular to that taken by the rest of the parade, homing in on a sack of feed sitting outside a general store.

Slocum had to pause as the man struggled to pull the huge bird back from what it must have seen as nothing short of paradise. But Slocum's gaze rose to the next street over. More animals paraded past, but these were more ordinary. He had seen their like in any of a dozen other circuses. What caught his eye was the trim young woman riding a prancing, large, white stallion.

She wore tight, bleached white leather britches that glistened in the hot Utah sun and made her appear as something ethereal. Her bare, tanned arms shone with a thin sheen of sweat; the fringed vest she wore rustled softly and caressed her supple body as she turned and moved; and the ten-gallon hat that would have looked ridiculous on another woman somehow seemed natural, normal. Long black hair flowed from under the hat and caught the wind, whipping like another circus banner. As arresting as her beauty, though, was the brace of pistols at her waist. She had them thrust into a broad red silk sash in the cross-draw fashion that Slocum himself preferred so he could draw while mounted.

Slocum had seen his share of men who wore their guns that way, and most of them were awkward, betraying their choice as pure affectation. Slocum had no sense that this woman wasn't able to draw and fire her pistols. And the rifle she held aloft showed silver dollars driven into the butt, another gimmick favored by men Slocum dismissed as greenhorns or blowhards. Something about the way the gun metal shone blue and well oiled told him this wasn't a stunt rifle. Like her sidearms, the rifle looked as if it had been used often and well.

The stallion reared but the woman kept it under perfect control. In spite of the parade of unusual animals from the Sells Brothers Circus still passing along the street in front of him, Slocum turned and went down the side street, passing the man struggling with his ostrich, and stopped at the corner of the next street. The people in this parade looked different, seedier, and their animals lacked the exotic appeal of those just one street over.

"Come free to our first performance," a man with a huge handlebar mustache cried, a heavy German accent almost obscuring his offer. "Come to the first performance of Baron Fenstermacher's Fabulous Continental Circus this very afternoon at the outskirts of town!"

Slocum turned and looked over his shoulder at the fancy livery and sharp appeal of the other circus' parade. He had to shake his head. Most towns went years between visits from a circus, and here this sleepy little Utah town was beset by two on the very same day. The people watching Baron Fenstermacher's parade numbered in the tens. The Sells Brothers Circus drew dozens, maybe hundreds. The children riding on the elephant's back crowed with glee. Their excited tale of riding that behemoth would bring droves of customers. Baron Fenstermacher had nothing of the sort to attract a crowd.

Slocum found himself watching the woman astride the powerful white stallion. She controlled her mount easily with only her legs; she was an experienced rider. Slocum wondered what she did in the circus. Almost as if on cue, the woman lowered her rifle and fired.

Slocum jumped as a pine knot exploded a few inches from his head. She had drilled the knot dead center.

"That's no lucky shot," she said in a voice that rolled to Slocum like wind through tall trees. "Come try your luck. Fifty dollars to the man who can outshoot me!"

She put her heels to the stallion's flanks and rode off in a cloud of dust that left Slocum choking. He wiped his lips to get the grit off and shook more grime from his duster. When the woman turned the corner with the rest of Baron Fenstermacher's paltry circus parade, Slocum decided it was high time to find the saloon and wet his whistle.

Search as he might, Slocum couldn't find a saloon or dance hall anywhere. He frowned and rubbed his leathery face in disgust. From the boardwalk came a polite cough to get his attention. An old man rocked back in a chair spat accurately into a brass cuspidor set beside him. When he had finished and was sure he had Slocum's attention, he said, "You got the look of a thirsty man."

"Need more than a pull of water," Slocum allowed.

"Thought as much. You might try the Blue Lantern Café out at the edge of town, out near where the circus put up its tents. Now I ain't sayin' you'd find some whiskey there, but then again, it don't hurt to look."

"Reckon not," Slocum said. He stood and waited for the rest of what the old man had to say. He'd seen folks like this often enough. They took their sweet time getting around to saying what was on their mind. It was like that with the old geezer.

"You might say that Matt told 'em you were okay," the man said.

"What would Matt consider to be fair payment for the introduction?" Slocum reached into his vest pocket and fingered the few small coins there. He wasn't sure what such information was worth, but he wasn't going to pay more than a dime for it. That much money would buy him a couple warm beers in most saloons.

"Don't much like this crud they sell for chawin' terbacky," the man said. "You got fixin's enough to share?"

Slocum had no problem with this. He tossed over a small pouch of tobacco and watched the man expertly roll a cigarette between his gnarled fingers. Then the old man rolled a second and a third, both vanishing into his shirt pocket. He tossed the pouch back.

"Much obliged. And mister, tell 'em out there that Tommy Joe sent you."

"You Tommy Joe or Matt?" Slocum was amused at this little deception.

"I'm the one what's got three good smokes," the old man said, settling back and aiming again for the cuspidor. Slocum touched the brim of his hat and walked off toward the boundary of the town. The Mormons didn't cotton much to drinking or smoking, though Slocum had known more than one who called himself a jack Mormon and partook of hard cider on occasion. It wasn't his call to pass judgment on other folks, but he wished they wouldn't pass judgment on him if he liked the taste of liquor. He wasn't the kind to have a half dozen wives, but he wasn't going to tell any of this community they couldn't.

The Blue Lantern Café was a clapboard structure that looked as if it might come tumbling down at any instant. Slocum made for it straight out, then slowed and finally stopped when he saw the circus tent and the crowd around it. The curious nature of the performers caused Slocum to forget his thirst for the moment.

Two men leaned on long rifles, but the third member of the sharpshooting team drew Slocum's undivided attention. The tow-headed boy couldn't have been older than fourteen or fifteen, yet he had the same flashing uniform as the other two. And if Slocum was any judge, the men deferred to the boy.

"We'll take on all comers," declared one man, "and we will prevail! We are members of the world famous Captain Bogardus Shooting Team, unparalleled in our skill. A dollar a match, and if you best us, we will give you ten dollars in gold!" The man strutted around like a peacock, holding aloft a leather pouch. Slocum didn't know if there was gold in it, and it didn't matter. A quick glance at the townspeople convinced him that no one could beat these professional marksmen. But the boy. Slocum wondered.

"What about him?" asked a curious onlooker. "The boy. He a member of your shooting team, too?"

The man turned and looked at the boy, who shyly shuffled one foot back and forth in the dirt and averted his eyes. Slocum knew an act when he saw it. He focused his attention on the man answering the question. He was tall, thin as a rail, and had a whipcord look to him that told of hard times and the molding of an even harder character. Slocum wasn't sure if he'd believe anything this man said— and he sure as hell wasn't likely to turn his back on him. This was the kind of man who'd as likely backshoot you as look at you.

"Billy is new to the team, a replacement for a ten-year veteran taken inexplicably ill, but we think he'll make a fine addition one day. Mr. Dellman and I are more experienced and will shoot to a match or two."

The lie came easily, but only Slocum recognized it for the come-on that it was.

"You mean I can challenge the boy and not you or the other fella?" the man in the crowd asked.

"Well . . ." The hesitation caused the townspeople to growl and rumble. The hatchet-faced sharpshooter cleared his throat and, as if relenting, said, "Very well. He *is* a member of the Bogardus Shooting Team. Billy, you've been challenged." He waved his hand, and the one named Dellman took the man's dollar.

"We'll shoot at glass balls filled with feathers. A hit is immediately obvious by the cloud of feathers floating down. You may pick your rifle from our rack or provide your own."

Slocum was amazed at the quickness of the pitch. Billy hefted his rifle, set his feet, and lifted his rifle to his shoulder, ready to shoot before the local man had chosen one of the other rifles in the rack.

"Start throwing. The first to miss loses!"

Dellman lofted a glass ball. Billy swung through, fired, and sent splinters of glass and chicken feathers showering down. A murmur passed through the crowd at such fine shooting. The local marksman spit on his finger, wiped off the front sight and swung the Winchester back and forth to get the feel of it. He planted his feet and nodded. A glass ball flashed skyward. The man shot and scored a direct hit. A cheer from the crowd went up.

Slocum paid little attention to either the crowd or their chosen champion. He was intent on Billy. There wasn't a hint of pressure affecting the youth. He was as cool as if he stood in a blizzard. He swung and hit the second ball as easily as he had the first. His attention shifted to the man who had done the hawking. He stood to one side, a sly grin on his face, as if he knew something no one else did.

Billy hit his fifth and sixth targets and hadn't even broken into a sweat, but the same couldn't be said for the man who had bet his dollar against ten in gold. He struggled to swing the rifle, and on his sixth shot he missed. The unscathed ball flashed brightly in the sunlight and arced downward to explode on the ground. A sigh passed through the crowd, and the ventured dollar was gone into the kitty of Captain Bogardus and the Sells Brothers Circus.

"Is there no one else who can give young Billy a run for his money? Surely the Utah frontier has produced a marksman of excellent caliber?" The hatchet-faced man laughed at his little joke.

"I'll give him a try," Slocum said, "but I want better odds."

"Better than ten dollars in gold versus a greenback dollar? Very well. We are new to the town and wish to entertain as well as win friends." The evil grin told Slocum these sharpshooters wanted nothing more than to win a few dollars and devil take the hindmost.

"One hundred gold against my dollar," Slocum said.

"Done!" The speed of agreement put Slocum on his guard. He had been in enough card games where marked decks were used to know the sensation of being had.

"Mind if I use my own rifle?"

"Not at all!" Again the quick agreement told Slocum something was wrong. He was going into a game with the odds stacked against him more than a hundred to one, and he couldn't figure out how. If the rifles had been tampered with, no one using them who didn't know their secret could hope to win, but Slocum's Winchester was perfectly sighted. He had been a sniper for the Confederacy during the war and had learned both proper care of a weapon and how to shoot straight and fast.

"Am I firing against you or the boy?" Slocum asked.

"Billy will take your money, sir, or I will. Your choice." The thin man bowed deeply, the smirk never leaving his lips. "I am Clay Wilkins, a member of the good captain's team for more than three years."

"The boy will do," Slocum said. "But I want someone from town to throw the balls. Like him." He turned and pointed to the man who had just lost. The smirk left Wilkins's face, and Slocum knew there was something wrong.

"The balls are fragile, and it takes a knowledgeable hand to throw them," Wilkins said. Slocum saw that arguing would get him nowhere. Even the man he had tried to enlist waved him on to begin the match. Slocum fetched his rifle and returned, spare cartridges weighing heavily in his pocket.

"Begin, Billy, and may the best man win!" Wilkins's smirk had returned. Whatever edge Bogardus's men had was once more in effect. Billy broke the first ball with no trouble. Then Slocum took his shot, following the rising glass target easily and smoothly pulling back the trigger just as his sights crossed the sphere. Glass and feathers showered down.

Fifteen minutes later, Billy continued to fire like a machine. The hot sun wore on Slocum, but he had been uncomfortable before. The lure of one hundred dollars kept him firing, even when he got a hang-fire and had to lever out the round and chamber another for a bull's-eye before the target dropped to the ground. A cheer went up from the crowd. From the corner of his eye Slocum saw Wilkins passing through the townspeople placing side bets.

Slocum kept firing but began to tire after eighty-four straight hits. His shoulder ached, and his eyes were blurring from the sun. He was sorry now that he hadn't gone to the Blue Lantern Café and had his drink first.

Billy kept firing as if he was a statue who only came to life when the feather-filled target launched upward and caught the sun. Slocum wondered if the boy was even human. He never looked anywhere but down the barrel of his rifle, and only occasionally turned to the small table at his side to reload.

Slocum's miss came with startling suddenness. He thought he had the glass ball in his sights, then he didn't, and the shot went wide by fractions of an inch.

"Go on, Billy. One more, just to show him how it's done," gloated Wilkins. Billy's next shot shattered the target as it had done before with agonizing regularity. Wilkins turned to the crowd, raised a thin arm to get their attention, and called out, "He was good to have lasted this long against a member of the Bogardus Shooting Team. But are you better? Who'll step up and—"

"I'll do it," came a voice Slocum thought he recognized. He turned and saw the woman from the other circus' parade pushing through the crowd. "I challenge you! And I'll beat you again, like I did in St. Louis!"

2

"No!"

Everyone in the gathered crowd turned and stared at Wilkins. The woman smiled at the hatchet-faced man's refusal, but Slocum saw there was no humor in her expression.

"What's wrong, Clay?" she asked with poisoned sweetness, her voice pitched loud enough for everyone to hear. "Afraid I will beat you *again*?" She bore down hard on the last word to emphasize that she had beaten one of Captain Bogardus's best.

"It's not that, Maddy."

"The name's Miss Scowcroft to you," she snapped.

Slocum saw that the animosity between the two ran deep. He stepped up, taking the woman's part in the argument. "Why not give her a chance?" he asked. "The boy's tired. Let's see how you do. You bragged that you were one of the best shots in the West."

"I am," Wilkins said sourly. "It's just that—"

"Afraid?" taunted someone in the crowd. "The boy might be the only one of 'em who can shoot worth a damn."

This idea passed through the crowd, and Wilkins saw that he was losing support fast. He cleared his throat, glared at Maddy Scowcroft, and then gave Slocum the same look. If Slocum had to choose camps, he decided he was on the right side in this fight. The woman pressed against his left arm. Tingles ran up and down from her nearness. He had seen his share of pretty women, but few matched this one. Maddy Scowcroft had a fire all too often lacking in truly beautiful women. Most relied only on their physical beauty. The tall, raven-haired, ebony-eyed woman was obviously a cut above that.

"Just you and me, Clay. One on one and to hell with any bet. This is for honor, not money."

"Afraid to put up money?" Wilkins asked nastily.

"It's not your money," Maddy said. "It's Bogardus's money, not yours," Maddy snapped. "And I don't have that kind of backing. You know the baron doesn't pay me enough for that."

"I'll see the bet," Slocum said quietly. "Even money. How much you willing to wager, Wilkins?"

Madeleine Scowcroft turned and looked Slocum over, as if seeing him for the first time. She finally asked in a whisper, "You got that much confidence in me?"

"Reckon so," Slocum said.

"Why? You've never seen me shoot."

"I like what I see," Slocum said. "You've got gumption." He turned and looked at Clay Wilkins, then added, "And I don't like what I see there."

"Fair enough. You won't regret it." Maddy unlimbered her rifle from her shoulder where she had it slung on a gaudy strap made from a strip of old Indian blanket. The silver dollars embedded in the stock gleamed in the sun. Slocum got a closer look at the rifle and nodded. It was a fine weapon, one lovingly tended. Wilkins grabbed the first rifle in the case and began loading.

"Any time you're ready," she said, setting her feet about a shoulder's width apart. Slocum appreciated the woman while she stood waiting. She was tall, almost matching his six feet, and she was in proportion without being heavy. To Slocum she said in a low voice, "My record is 983 targets before a miss."

Slocum whistled through his teeth since he hadn't reached 100 before giving out. There wasn't a hint of boasting to the woman's claim. She made it as factually as if she had told him the sun had come up that morning. The silence that had fallen on the crowd was shattered when Maddy spun and fired, Wilkins's assistant hurrying the first target to catch her off guard.

"They're low-down snakes in the grass," she said off-handedly, levering another round into the rifle's firing chamber. "You got to watch every sneaky move, but any snake can be beat fair and square if you're better."

Wilkins fired and got his first target. Maddy's second followed almost immediately. She easily blasted it into dust and feathers. Slocum stepped back to let the two contestants have plenty of room for their match. Maddy didn't work as the young Billy had, like a machine. She appraised the target and worked off her judgment. Clay Wilkins tried to follow his young partner's example, but Slocum saw this wasn't working. Emotion flowed across the man's thin face, and it wasn't pretty. Whatever Madeleine had done to him before, it had left a deep wound he meant to avenge.

The crowd whispered among themselves as the count mounted. Maddy showed no hint of the strain as the number of successfully broken targets approached one hundred and then surpassed it, but Wilkins did. He sweat profusely, and his hand began to shake as he reached for new rounds for his rifle. Slocum remembered how his own shoulder had begun to hurt after thirty rounds. By now Clay Wilkins ought to be hurting.

For that matter, so should the woman, but she was falling into an easy rhythm of aiming and firing that belied the physical strain. This was something she had done often, and Slocum had to admit she did it far better than he did. Turning his attention from her trim figure and flashing rifle, he studied Wilkins's cohorts. Billy watched with the rapt fascination of a boy watching his elder perform a new and marvelous feat. But the man throwing the glass targets held Slocum's attention. Something about the way Dellman selected the spheres wasn't quite right.

Maddy kept breaking the soaring targets, as did Wilkins. But the man was beginning to flag. Slocum glanced at him, then studied the assistant throwing the targets. He saw that Dellman took Wilkins's targets from one box and Maddy's from another. Slocum moved closer and read the legend on the sides of the boxes.

Both had been produced at the Bogardus Firearms Factory.

"Don't do that," Dellman snapped when Slocum reached for one of the targets in the box supplying Wilkins.

"Why not?"

"You're breaking my concentration. Don't do nothing to—"

Slocum ignored the man and grabbed one of Wilkins's targets. A slight crack showed in the glass. He dropped it and it shattered. He then rooted through the box of targets Maddy was being given. Not a one had so much as a slight flaw.

Slocum shrugged his shoulders and moved so that his hand rested on the ebony handle of his Colt.

"Switch," he ordered. "Give these to Wilkins." He pointed to the box from which Maddy's targets came. The crack he had seen might mean nothing. A target here and there would be flawed in any shipment, but he didn't think it worked that way. Maddy had to hit every glass ball squarely to scatter the contents. All Wilkins had to do was nick the already cracked glass to score a hit.

"Mister, don't," Dellman pleaded. "You don't know how mad he can get. Clay's a holy terror."

"Do it," Slocum said in a cold voice.

"Hold up!" Wilkins shouted, seeing the problem. Sweat ran down his face in rivers. He put down his rifle, wincing as he accidentally touched the hot barrel. "What's wrong?"

"Clay, he wants to change targets." Dellman almost pleaded with Slocum to reconsider. To those in the crowd, this seemed to be a frivolous request. But if anyone examined the targets and saw the trick, they'd rip Wilkins limb from limb for cheating.

"We can't," Wilkins began, then saw he couldn't argue the point.

"What do you say we call the match a draw. You both hit the same number, haven't you?" Slocum said.

"I'm one up on him," Maddy said, not understanding the problem.

"One more, then," Slocum said. "From *this* box." He pointed to the unflawed targets. Clay Wilkins began to sweat even more.

"I can beat him," protested Maddy. "Don't call this off. I can beat him!"

"One more," Slocum said. "Do it." His hand twitched slightly toward the worn handle of his six-shooter. Wilkins knew firearms and knew a well used one when he saw it. Slocum's cold green eyes and implacable gaze gave him no choice.

"One more," he said.

The pressure was on Wilkins to hit a perfect target. His hand shook when he lifted his rifle and signaled for the target. Dellman tossed it and by the barest amount Wilkins made the shot. He almost slumped to the ground with relief when a few feathers drifted down.

"A draw," Slocum said, taking Maddy's arm before she could complain. Louder, for the crowd's benefit, he said, "Come on over to Baron Fenstermacher's Continental Circus for more fine shooting."

"That's Baron Fenstermacher's *Fabulous* Continental Circus," Maddy corrected, "and our first show is free. Tell your friends!"

She let Slocum pull her away from the crowd to the relative seclusion of a side street before jerking away and flaring, "Why'd you stop the match! I could have taken him! I did it before. He's not that good."

"He was cheating," Slocum said coldly. He explained how she got perfect targets and those Wilkins fired at were at the point of falling apart just from the aerial toss.

"Why that son of a bitch! He—" She sputtered, trying vainly to come up with an appropriate description.

"Let it be," Slocum advised. "You got publicity for your show at Wilkins's expense. There'll be other days, and maybe you can beat him fairly then."

"Even cheating I could have beaten him," Maddy said angrily. Then she took a deep breath. Slocum appreciated the sight of the rise and fall of her breasts under the tight leather vest. "I'm being ungracious. Thank you for helping me like that. And you're one hell of a sharpshooter yourself."

"Not in your league," Slocum said. With a wry grin he added, "And not in the boy's, either."

"If he was using the broken targets, you don't know if you could have bested him."

"He's good," Slocum said sincerely, knowing it was the truth. He had seldom seen anyone shoot with the confidence or accuracy that Billy had. Clay Wilkins wasn't anywhere near as good, but Slocum wasn't sure about Madeleine Scowcroft. She had acted as if a hundred targets was just a warm-up for her. Neither she nor Billy needed broken targets for their fine work.

"Why are you taking their side? I thought you wanted to help out?" She looked at him with her bottomless midnight eyes, accusing him of sins beyond compare.

"Don't have anything against them, except maybe for Wilkins," Slocum said. "I don't take kindly to being cheated, but the boy's good. You can see it."

"As good as you if he didn't have an advantage?" Maddy had cut right to the heart of the problem.

Slocum only shrugged. There wasn't any way of telling without a rematch, and his shoulder hurt like a hill of ants had made it their new home. Even slight movement sent ripples of pain into his body. It took more than good reflexes and a sharp eye for the kind of shooting these people enjoyed.

"What caused the rivalry between you and the people at Sells Brothers Circus?" he asked. Maddy stiffened as she walked, the change in her gait instantly obvious. Feelings ran deep over something.

"They wanted to buy out Baron Fenstermacher two years back, and he turned them down. The Sells brothers are honest showmen and deliver a good product." She tried not to be too obvious as she looked toward the compound where Jumbo, the lions and tigers, the strange bird whose name Slocum had already forgotten, and the other beasts were caged. "They always go top dollar on their beasts and trainers, too."

"It's just the humans in their circus you don't cotton much to, is that it?"

"That's it. And most of them are fine folks. It's just the ones like Clay Wilkins that get my goat."

"What about this Captain Bogardus? I don't remember hearing anything of him. Is this some made-up character?"

"The captain?" Maddy laughed without humor. "No, he's real enough. Believe me, Adam Bogardus is all too real."

"And you have a quarrel with him, too," Slocum finished.

"He's not half the sharpshooter his publicity makes him out to be. I could beat him in any honest match, and he knows it. He threw in with the Sells brothers and is living off their money by hustling audiences. Wilkins is only part of the scheme. Bogardus travels throughout the West making himself out to be the great gun-handler. Why, he said he hit 995 out of a 1000 glass balls at the California Sporting Club last year."

Slocum frowned. He had heard something about such a shooting match, but he thought it had been back in '77.

"Winchester gave him two of the Model 1873s with rose-wood stocks," Maddy went on. "He always shoots .44-40 rounds with 200-grain bullets."

Slocum rubbed his shoulder as he considered what he would have felt like if he'd fired his rifle a thousand times rather than less than a hundred. It took a real expert to keep at a match that long.

"Doc Carver's better, maybe the best," she said. "He's beaten Bogardus time and again. I saw him shoot once. Stands six-foot-four and weighs two-fifty if he weighs an ounce. An impressive figure. The Brulé Sioux call him Evil Spirit because he never misses, and the Santee Sioux named him the Spirit Gun. Now Carver's a *real* sharpshooter, not a puffed-up fraud."

Slocum had watched the woman throughout her dia-tribe against Adam Bogardus. Whatever it was between her and the self-proclaimed master marksman of the West, it went deeper than publicity claims. They turned away from the Sells Brothers Circus encampment. Slocum's attention turned back to the woman. For a few minutes she seemed unaware of his appreciative gaze, but when she saw his admiration she smiled and lifted her chin slightly, almost strutting along. She appreciated him as much as he did her.

"The brothers tried to buy out the baron, but he's from a fine old Continental family. He wouldn't have any of it," Maddy said. "You'll like him."

The compound for the baron's circus was entirely different, much smaller and almost a parody of the Sells Brothers Circus. The variety of animals was lacking. And then Slocum heard a trumpeting that shook the very ground under his boots.

"What was that?" His hand had flashed to his pistol, but he knew anything making a noise that loud wouldn't be frightened by the threat of a six-shooter.

Maddy laughed and brushed back a strand of her black hair as it fell forward into her eyes. She tossed her head slightly and pointed. "That's Trajan, our answer to Jumbo."

Slocum could hardly believe his eyes. The elephant he had seen in the Sells Brothers Circus parade had been immense. The animal poking its head through the circus tent was half again the size of Jumbo.

"Trajan stands damn near nine feet tall," came a voice behind Slocum. "You ever see anything like him before, mister?"

"No, can't say I have," Slocum said, looking the man over as if he was some demon from hell. The slight man was dressed in tights that showed his wiry physique to its best effect. "Name's John Slocum." He thrust out his hand and waited.

"This is The Great Morelli," introduced Maddy. "He's our funambulist."

Slocum hesitated. He didn't know what the woman was talking about. Then he said, "I hope that's not contagious, whatever it is."

Morelli laughed and said, "I'm the tightwire walker. I've been with the baron for well nigh four years now. He gave me a job when I needed it, and I owe him everything."

Slocum wondered why the man unburdened himself with the tale of his life so quickly. Maddy took his arm and shut off any comment on his part. Morelli touched his finger to his forehead, gave a mock half-salute, and strolled away, whistling off-key.

"He's taken more than one fall from the highwire." She tapped the side of her head to show where The Great Morelli had landed and how it had affected him. "But he's a good performer, and the children love his antics on the wire."

"You mean he walks a wire strung between two posts?" Slocum shook his head. He'd heard of such things but had never seen anyone fool enough to do it.

"That, among other things. We all double up on jobs. We're not like the Sells brothers who have a hundred or more people on the payroll."

"What other jobs do you have, besides sharpshooter?" Visions of what such a lovely woman might do flashed through Slocum's mind. He was disappointed at the answer he got.

"I sell tickets, see to preparing the handbills advertising the show, things like that." Maddy smiled wryly and said, "I'm one of the few performers who can read, write, and cipher."

Before Slocum could say a word, a horrible screaming came from inside the circus tent.

"No, not again," gasped Maddy. "Morelli is also our fire-eater, and sometimes sets himself on fire. Grab a bucket and follow me."

Slocum scooped up a bent red fire bucket near the entrance to the circus tent and rushed inside, ready to douse anyone he saw who was on fire. He paused when Maddy held up her hand. The man doing the screaming wasn't Morelli, but a short, stout man with a long handlebar mustache. He was dressed in a bright red coat with gold frogs and epaulets dancing with intricate braid as he moved. The man stormed back and forth, smashing his right fist into the palm of his other hand with a sound like breaking boards.

"We are ruined," he cried. "Ruined beyond any possible redemption. How could this have happened to us?"

"The baron?" asked Slocum.

Maddy only nodded numbly.

"What's happened?" he asked. The baron was in no condition to answer. Maddy hurried to speak with a portly man who wore a distraught expression. They talked for several minutes. Slocum drifted closer to hear what they were saying.

"Mr. Slocum, this is Madison Kincaid, the circus' business manager."

"The news is not favorable," Kincaid said, shaking his head and looking at the baron.

"Our railroad cars," the woman said in a choked voice. "We've lost them. We're trapped in this nowhere Utah town!"

3

"I don't understand," Slocum said. He looked from the woman to the heavy set business manager and back. "What do you mean the cars are gone? Just disappeared?"

"Gone, I say. They have passed us by. They rolled on to the next stop and stranded us in this terrible town!" Kincaid's lips thinned to a tight line. He closed his eyes for a moment when the baron stormed over and planted his feet firmly. Slocum had seen foreigners get too close when they talked. The baron thrust his face less than three inches from Kincaid's, as if daring the businessman to say a word. Kincaid returned the baron's hot gaze and kept quiet.

Baron Fenstermacher was beside himself with a mixture of anger and worry. He slapped his hand against his thigh, started to rage some more, then pulled away and went off, grumbling as he went. Morelli followed, as did several others, to see what they could do to calm their employer. Maddy hung back, wanting to go with the circus owner but staying at Slocum's side.

"This might destroy us," she said. "We need the cars to move the circus. If the railroad has sent them on, it'll be days before we can arrange for others. And not every freight car can house Trajan."

Outside the tent, the huge elephant trumpeted, as if in sympathy with the circus' problems. Slocum hoped that

21

the elephant didn't get as upset as the baron had and go storming off. There wouldn't be much more than kindling left of the town.

"This won't affect your show tonight, will it?"

"No," Kincaid said, "but we have already made commitments in other towns along the line. If we don't show up, they won't trust us." He made a wry face and said, "As if they do anyway. There's hardly a town in this country that cottons much to show people. They think anyone travelling around in a railroad car, staying a day or two and then moving on has to be some kind of sneak thief." The bitterness in his voice told of more than the life of a gypsy. He snorted like a pig missing its wallow, pushed past Slocum, and hurried after the baron.

"Kincaid's right," Maddy said, duplicating the tone. "We can't just stay. They won't tolerate us more than a day or two. No decent folks will."

"You lose somebody who didn't want to move on with you?" Slocum hazarded. He saw by Maddy's expression that he was right. "Then he's a damned fool."

"You flatter me," she said.

"Reckon I've been at the same place myself a time or two," Slocum said, thinking back to the many women he had left behind him—and those who had left him because they couldn't tolerate his footloose ways. A time or two he had thought of settling down, but he had never had reason enough to do it. He had been shot up something fierce during the war, and by the time he had healed, his parents back in Calhoun, Georgia, were long dead. His brother Robert had fallen during Pickett's Charge, leaving him sole owner of the Slocum homestead. He had regained his strength just in time to be presented with a bogus bill for unpaid taxes assessed by a carpetbagger judge out to start his own stud farm.

Slocum had resisted, and the judge had ridden out to the farm one day with his hired gun. Only John Slocum had ridden away, leaving behind two fresh graves. Ever since, Wanted posters had dogged his trail. The law never forgave a judge-killer, even when the killing had been deserved.

Keeping ahead of bounty hunters, the law, and simple notoriety along with his desire always to drift on to see what lay beyond the next rise had kept Slocum in the saddle. He understood Madeleine Scowcroft's problems, traveling with the circus as she did.

"You're packing a powerful lot of memories," she said.

"Nothing I can't live with," he said brusquely. "What are you going to do if you can't get the circus to the next town?"

She shook her head, causing soft, long hair to float like a dark cloud around her lovely face. "Don't know. But the circus is important to us. We can't let a mix-up do us in."

"The baron is skating on thin ice financially, isn't he?"

"You don't miss much, John," she said. "Baron Fenstermacher came from a rich family, but he sank most of his fortune into the circus over the years, and frankly, we haven't been getting the best billings lately. Our acts leave, we don't get invited to the bigger cities, animals get sick and die and can't be replaced."

"Competition is fierce," Slocum said, his mind wandering along other routes.

"The Sells Brothers Circus will draw more money from the town than we will because they have better animals."

"Animals is right," Slocum said. "You need to get ready for your afternoon performance. The shootout with Wilkins might get you a few more paying customers."

"Our first show is always free," Maddy said. "We try to give the townspeople something special to thank them for letting us set up. Heaven knows there are some towns that won't let our kind inside the city limits."

"Good for business later on, too," Slocum said, still distracted. "Word gets around who has the most interesting show." For a moment, his gaze fastened on hers. She smiled, and this was reward enough for Slocum's small compliment. "I've got to see to a few things in town."

"See you later, John?"

"Wild horses couldn't keep me away," he promised. Slocum turned to go when he felt her hand grip his arm.

He stopped and was surprised when she kissed him lightly on the cheek.

"Thanks," she said.

"For what?"

"For keeping me from making a fool of myself in the match with Clay Wilkins. It never occurred to me he'd cheat. To be beaten in front of that crowd would have guaranteed we'd never see anyone show up for our performances."

"My pleasure," Slocum said.

Maddy started to say something more, blushed, and then spun and hurried off, leaving him alone in the circus tent. He looked up at the huge tent and wondered what it would be like to be in the large center ring, all eyes on him. He shuddered at the notion. That wasn't any kind of life he could appreciate, not fully. He'd leave it for lovely women like Madeleine Scowcroft and crazy men who ate fire and walked on thin wires as The Great Morelli did.

He checked his six-shooter, making sure all six chambers carried a charge. He usually rode with the hammer resting on an empty chamber to prevent accidental discharge. Now that he was among men rather than rattlers and other natural varmints, he might need the extra round. Satisfied that he was armed for his mission, Slocum exited the circus tent, gave Trajan a wide berth, and made his way toward the Blue Lantern Café to slake his thirst.

He went into the dimly lit café and looked around. To the rear was a closed door. He went to it and knocked. From inside he heard a mumbled voice ask, "What is it?"

"Tommy Joe said you might have something for me."

The door opened a crack and two bleary eyes peered out to study him for a few seconds. Whatever decided the man on the other side, Slocum couldn't tell. It might have been mention of the old man's name, or it might just be that he looked like a cowboy out to wet his whistle and not a crusading Mormon bent on shutting down all saloons within the town's boundary. He slipped into the small room where four others sat around a pickle barrel, using its top as their table. A single bottle of whiskey stood in the middle of the barrel's top. However long the men had been here, they had almost finished the liquor. Slocum figured he was lucky to arrive when he did. He wasn't sure if there'd be a second bottle.

"Looks good," he said, indicating the whiskey. One man who looked more like a pine weasel than a human wiped off a shot glass and silently handed it to Slocum. No one offered to pour for him so he grabbed the bottle by the neck and splashed out a healthy amount into the glass. He downed it and almost gagged.

"Smooth, ain't it?" asked the weaselly barkeep.

"Yeah, real smooth," Slocum choked out. He kept from coughing. Swallowing sandpaper would have been easier and a sight more refreshing. He poured a second and worked on it more carefully, letting it work its way down his throat eventually to pool hotly in his belly.

"Set a spell," offered one of the men at the pickle barrel who had been silent up till now. "Don't see many strangers here. Tommy Joe don't trust many folks who are just passin' through."

"Tommy Joe and I hit it off," Slocum allowed. "I'm not especially planning on staying here," he said, trying vainly to remember the Utah town's name, "but I heard tell the train's gone already. A whole damned train of empty cars just went rolling on through."

"Yep, that they did," said the barkeep. "The engineer was pissed off, he was, but for the money he got, he could afford to swallow a bit of bile."

"What do you mean?" Slocum eyed the bottle and wondered if his throat would stand another shot. He decided to take the chance. This was worse than trade whiskey, even if it didn't have a few rusty nails added for body and a hefty shot of nitric acid in it to give a mule's kick.

"They got all tangled up at the railhead," the barkeep said, the others listening as intently as Slocum to the gossip. There wasn't much to do in town.

"I still don't follow you," Slocum said. He had jumped ahead and thought he knew what the bartender was getting at, but he wanted it spelled out to be sure.

"That shooter fellow, the one with the sneaky look, he paid the engineer to just steam on through and not stop. Can't figure out why since the conductor told me they was here to pick up a circus."

Slocum saw that the men had confused the Sells Brothers Circus and Baron Fenstermacher's show. Everything Maddy had said was true about the larger circus siphoning off both money and spectators. And it seemed Wilkins was willing to go to greater lengths to make sure the baron failed.

"You're the one what shot it out with the boy and lost, ain't you?" asked another of the men who had been quietly drinking and belching.

"He's good," Slocum said, putting his glass down on the pickle barrel. "If he keeps at it, he might be as good a sharpshooter as there's ever been."

He left when the men got to lying about their own prowess, both with a gun and sexually, and that of others they had seen. None of them mentioned Madeleine Scowcroft or how she had matched Wilkins earlier. All they remembered was the fourteen-year-old outshooting a seasoned man like Slocum.

Outside the Blue Lantern, hot sun and wind had given way to twilight and a cold wind blowing across the foothills of the Wasatch Mountains. Slocum stretched and began wandering the streets, not knowing what he was looking for. If he hadn't ridden in earlier, he would have thought the place was a ghost town. The coming of the circus—the circuses—had sapped everyone's will to work. This was an unexpected holiday for them in the middle of a week.

He glanced toward the side of town where the Sells Brothers Circus was in full swing. Barkers harangued the throng and urged them inside for just a dime. Slocum kept walking and saw a more modest crowd outside the baron's circus tent. Even free, the baron couldn't pull the interest shown in the larger circus. One glance at Maddy riding her white stallion prancing around outside the tent convinced Slocum that those over at the Sells Brothers Circus were fools. It was worth the price of damned near any admission to watch her ride—and it didn't take a former sniper to appreciate her expertise with that rifle of hers.

She saw him and waved. He touched the brim of his hat and watched as she galloped off to find more folks willing to watch the first show for free. Slocum went into the tent and found a spot at the top on the rickety bleachers. The day's heat lingered here but he didn't mind. The show was just getting under way. Baron Fenstermacher cut a fine figure in his fancy ringmaster duds, and his slight accent lent an air of the Continent to whatever he said. The first act was The Great Morelli walking on a wire strung between two poles. Slocum didn't know how it was possible for anyone to walk on such a thin string, but Morelli had no trouble except for the parts of his act when he built up some suspense with false starts and apparent unbalance.

The next act was Madeleine Scowcroft. She came riding hellbent for leather into the center ring and began firing at targets placed along the side opposite the spectators using the six-shooters she carried cross-draw in her red sash.

Slocum marvelled at her expertise. It seemed that the woman couldn't miss, as if each bullet was following a string tied to her target. Clay pipes exploded, holes appeared in paper bulls-eyes, and whiskey bottle after bottle blasted apart under her leaden onslaught. And she did it all while riding at a full gallop. The distance wasn't great, but Slocum knew how hard it was to fire accurately from horseback. He always tried to get his horse as calm as possible before squeezing off a shot, and then it was almost impossible to make a good second shot. The horse would start crow-hopping from the sudden noise.

Morelli returned to eat fire and the clowns cavorted, but the centerpiece of Baron Fenstermacher's Fabulous Continental Circus was the elephant Trajan. When the animal lumbered into the ring, a hush fell over the crowd. Then excited whispers started as the beast went through its simple act.

"Like the show?"

Slocum jumped. He had been paying too much attention to the elephant and not enough to what was going on around him. Maddy had climbed the bleachers and sat down beside him, and he hadn't noticed.

"Surely do like your sharpshooting. Where'd you learn to shoot like that?"

She shrugged, and he knew whatever she told him was going to be a lie—or at least not the truth. "Just came to me, I reckon," she said. Maddy turned in the hard seat and stared at him with her fathomless dark eyes. "You planning on staying around here a while longer?"

Slocum shook his head. He never planned on staying anywhere too long.

"You're a fine shot. We can use another sharpshooter for the circus. We could do an act together, you on the ground and me riding. It doesn't pay much, the baron doesn't have much money, but if you don't have a job and—" She bit off the rest of the torrent of words and turned to watch as Trajan made his exit. "Sorry, I do carry on. You've probably got other plans."

"Nothing that can't be changed," Slocum said, not having any plans at all other than to keep riding west to see what he could see. "I'm not the showman you are. I don't know if anyone would pay to see me shoot a few whiskey bottles."

Maddy laughed harshly. "They're not paying much to see anything we have to offer. This is all we can draw with a *free* show. The crowd will be smaller tonight when they have to pay to get in."

"Nobody values what they get too lightly," Slocum said.

"Maybe so, but the baron's got to do something to attract people. Handbills don't work too good." She let out a huge sigh. "And getting on to our next engagement is going to be hard."

"I'll think on it for a spell," Slocum said.

"You didn't even ask what the baron would pay."

"That's not the important part," Slocum said.

"Show business," Maddy muttered. "Can't leave it once you get infected by it." She stood suddenly and hurried off, leaving Slocum to consider the unexpected offer. He hadn't been looking for a job—he still had a considerable sum riding in his pocket—but he remembered going to the circus with his pa and his brother when he was nine or ten. Ever since, it had been in the back of his mind that this was about the finest show he had ever seen.

Never in his wildest dreams had he thought he'd be asked to be part of such a spectacle, especially by a stunningly beautiful woman.

4

The evening performance ended a little after ten, and it had gone as Maddy had predicted. There were few paying customers, most of the town being lured away by the competing circus. Slocum had stayed on the bleacher seat long after Maddy had made her offer to join the circus, thinking hard. He knew that Clay Wilkins had bribed the engineer to take the baron's railroad cars on to the next stop along the line. It wasn't enough that the Sells Brothers Circus attracted the bulk of the town with their superior animal acts. Wilkins had to be a sneaky, underhanded, low-down bastard. From what Maddy had said about his boss, Adam Bogardus, the man might be getting some encouragement, not that Slocum thought he needed much. The feral look in Wilkins's eyes told of someone never to turn your back on.

He had stayed on the bleachers through the evening performance and had finally come to his conclusion. Every young boy's dream is to run off and join the circus. Slocum had been invited. He had to admit that the source of the invitation counted as much in his decision as anything else. Madeleine Scowcroft was easy on the eyes and didn't seem to find Slocum hard to look at, either.

Trajan trumpeted and vanished through the tent's canvas folds before Slocum stood and made his way to the sawdust-covered center ring. Morelli put away the implements of his fire-eating act, having combined this with his wire-walking as part of the finale. A few animal handlers stood around, muttering among themselves, and Baron Fenstermacher scribbled wildly on a small pad of paper. Slocum went to where Maddy gentled her stallion, patting it on the nose and feeding it lumps of sugar.

"Hello, John. I'm surprise you're still here. I thought you'd have been long gone by now."

"Who can resist the lure of the big top?" Slocum asked. "If your offer still stands, I'll take it."

"You will?" Her eyes widened, and she let out a whoop of joy. She threw her arms around his neck and almost bowled him over as she hugged him. "We surely can use a man like you." Her dark eyes said even more, but Slocum didn't want to read too much into that gaze. He might be kidding himself about her intentions.

"You talk this over with your boss?"

"The baron? Come on over, and let's see what he has to say."

Slocum trailed Maddy and waited patiently while the baron rattled off commands to the animal handlers. A few mumbled but all left. Only then did Maddy speak to the short man.

"Baron, this is John Slocum. He's the one I told you about, the one who went a hundred shots with Billy this afternoon."

"So, a sharpshooter, eh?" The baron jerked Slocum's hand up and down like the handle on a pump. "You will join us. This is good. Maddy can use an assistant."

Slocum started to protest, but the woman held up her hand. The smile on her lips told him that it wouldn't matter what the baron thought. Slocum wasn't angling for top billing, anyway. He had met damned few men who could outshoot him, and Maddy might be the first woman.

"Baron, is this smart?" asked Kincaid. "We don't have the money to take on more hands now."

"It is no worry, my good friend. We must overcome our problem with the trains," the baron said.

"We are stranded," Kincaid said. "No way of moving on."

Slocum studied the man. Kincaid didn't seem that upset over the prospect of being marooned until another train could be sent along the line. Slocum wondered why. The baron startled him with a sudden shout.

"We do not need these noisy rolling cars. No! We will do it as we used to, in the old days, in the old country."

"What are you planning?" Slocum asked.

"The baggage will go ahead on wagons. Now they will go since they travel more slowly than the animals. By the time we are to be in the next venue, both baggage and animals will arrive." The baron was waxing enthusiastic over his plan.

"We can't afford this, Baron," protested Kincaid.

Slocum heard the clatter of wagons outside the tent. Someone yelled, and Maddy motioned for Slocum to leave the big top. He saw the center pole begin to wobble back and forth as the tent pegs were pulled out. The entire tent would be on the ground within a minute. The men struggling with packing handled the vast expanse of canvas with skill. Slocum watched while they got sections of it onto wagons.

"Madison," the baron said to his manager, "you worry too much about these things." Fenstermacher cut off further argument. "They will leave now with other things," he said in an excited voice. "We will show them how a real circus operates!" He wandered off, shouting orders and getting the animal handlers to look after their caged wards.

"So he's going ahead by road," Slocum said. "Is it possible?"

"More than possible. I've never done it, but the baron has," Maddy told him. "What do you think they did in the days before railroads?"

"Never thought much on it. I'm usually in the saddle, so it's not out of the question to travel that way, except it'd be hard for the caged animals."

"Not as hard as you'd think," she said. "I've got to get

my gear packed. Unless the baron says different, we'll be leaving in the morning with the animals." Maddy looked at him and started to say something more, then stopped, chewed on her lower lip and finally hurried off. Slocum wasn't exactly sure what he was supposed to do, so he went and helped the half dozen men struggling to get the tent and other baggage into wagons. A little after midnight he wiped his forehead clear of sweat and watched the wagons leave. As heavily laden as they were, it'd take two days for them to reach Forlorn, Utah, the next stop. And the animals, being lighter, could travel faster in their wagons and take only a day and a half.

Slocum brought his horse around and tethered it with some of the less exotic beasts, where it contentedly nibbled at the hay. He then found a place to spread his bedroll and lay down, but sleep took a while to find him. He kept thinking of Madeleine Scowcroft.

The traveling went more smoothly than Slocum would have thought. They got through noon the next day without any problems. Slocum spent half his time riding ahead to scout the trail for the short caravan, then returning to tell the baron about any possible difficulty. Each time he returned, he felt Maddy watching him, but she never came up to talk. Slocum wondered why she kept her distance, but he wasn't going to press the matter. The job he had assigned to himself was time consuming and necessary if the circus was to make their next performance on time.

"So this road is growing steeper, eh?" the baron said, stroking his walrus mustache. "This will be the big problem. The mules tire of the long haul."

Slocum looked back at the towering elephant. "Any way you could hitch Trajan up to the wagons? An animal that size ought to be able to pull the entire bunch of wagons all by himself."

"That is a fine idea. In India, elephants are used for such things. They drag heavy logs and do other work. But they cannot jump. Are there the ravines?"

"Ravines?" Slocum didn't know what to say. The Utah countryside was filled with arroyos. "Everywhere."

"The elephant cannot cross anything it is unable to step over. You must be sure there are no deep, wide cuts in the road if we are to use the elephant."

"Don't rightly remember any such problem, but I'll check to be sure. How wide is too wide?"

The baron didn't know. He motioned, and Trajan's handler hurried over to his employer. They talked in German for some time, Slocum unable to follow a word of their conversation. Baron Fenstermacher finally said, "Andre says nothing broader than four feet."

"How deep?"

"Inches," was all he said.

Slocum wheeled his horse and started back to his scouting. At the top of the long rise the circus was struggling up, he turned and looked back to see Maddy astride her flashing white stallion. He waved, and she returned the greeting. Slocum couldn't figure her out. The night before he had expected something more than he had gotten from her. She had been eager for him to join the circus and then had turned aloof. Or had she? The demands of getting the circus packed and on the road were a world different from loading animals and baggage onto a railroad freight car.

Slocum rode for twenty minutes, then stopped and stood in the stirrups. Something bothered him, and he couldn't put his finger on exactly what it was. The day was hot, and insects buzzed eagerly around his face, hungrily seeking his sweat. Not much in the way of wildlife stirred during the day, but he saw plenty of evidence of rabbits and other small critters poking their heads from hidden burrows.

He tried to listen for unusual sounds, but the whistling wind kept him from identifying the source of his uneasiness. He hadn't seen any spot in the road that the balky elephant couldn't navigate, but there was something more. The gunshot confirmed what had been bothering Slocum. The baron and his circus weren't alone on this desolate road. The wagons with their baggage must have passed successfully, but the road agents working this stretch had come along at the worst possible time.

More gunshots made Slocum put his heels into his sorrel's sides. The animal struggled to give as much speed as Slocum demanded. He reined back when he got to a rise looking back down the road. Highwaymen had attacked the circus just where they couldn't find cover.

"Get 'em," came the cry from downslope. "Leave the big gray thing for me, though. I wanna be the one to shoot it!"

Slocum yanked his Winchester from its sheath and levered a shell into its firing chamber. Using only his knees, Slocum tightened the grip on his horse's flanks. He rose up slightly, aimed, and fired. An outlaw's hat went flying into the air. The road agent jumped up in surprise and spun to face this unexpected attack. Another shot sent the outlaw flying face forward into the dust.

Slocum didn't stop to wonder who had fired the killing shot. He was busy trying to quiet his sorrel to get off a second shot. The horse pawed at the ground a mite, then settled down. Slocum fired again, and this time he hit pay dirt. Another outlaw jerked as a bullet fatally ripped through his body, then dropped to his knees. For a moment, the man hung there, then crumpled to the side.

A fusillade of bullets drove the outlaws for cover. A third one was winged, and Slocum might have put a hole in a fourth, though he wasn't sure. The attack that had started on a defenseless circus caravan had turned deadly—for the road agents themselves.

"Run!" Slocum heard one highwayman yell. "There's a whole damn army shootin' at us!"

Slocum fired in measured cadence, making every round count. He didn't hit anyone else, but the flying lead added speed to the retreating bandits. He saw the one who had wanted to kill Trajan jump into the saddle and bend low to keep from being hit. Slocum took special aim and squeezed, only to have the hammer fall on an empty chamber. He hadn't been counting and had run through the rifle's magazine. He cursed as he started reloading.

The outlaw saw that Slocum had momentarily run dry and got careless. He straightened in the saddle and swung his six-shooter around for a shot. At this range it would have been the shot of the century, but Slocum started for cover. When the report rang loud and clear, though, he knew it wasn't from any handgun. A rifle had fired.

It had fired and taken the road agent out of his saddle. The man lay face up in the gorge, not moving. Slocum saw the flash of silver in the distance and knew that Maddy had made another fantastic shot with her Winchester. He hadn't been in much danger—certainly not as much as the careless outlaw. Still, Slocum appreciated both her skill and how she had saved him from dodging bullets.

The fleeing highwaymen were beyond both his range and skill, but he fired a few rounds to keep them moving away. Only when they had vanished did he guide his horse back down the road, riding slowly to keep from being bushwhacked by someone in the baron's circus. It hardly surprised him when he discovered that only he and Maddy were armed. The two of them were the sole reason the road agents had been driven off.

"Everybody all right?" Slocum yelled, just to be sure someone didn't have a hideout gun and nervously use it on him as he rode up. The pounding of hooves marked Maddy's arrival. She held her fancy Winchester, the silver dollars embedded in the stock gleaming in the setting sun.

"Everyone is alive," the baron said. "More than this, none of the animals was harmed."

As if to protest human behavior, Trajan trumpeted loudly and began tossing its huge head from side to side. Its trainer Andre tried to soothe it, speaking a steady stream of German, then switching to French. Slocum wondered if the elephant understood any English.

"We've got to get them, John," Maddy cried, out of breath from her frantic ride. "Let's go!"

"Whoa, wait," Slocum said, reaching out and grabbing the reins of her horse. He was almost pulled from the saddle before she dug in her heels and stopped the powerful stallion. "That's better," he said. "There's no reason to go gallivanting off after them."

"They're criminals. They tried to kill us!"

"We gave better than we got," he said. "Those owlhoots aren't going to stop riding until they find a saloon and can drink away their fright."

"He is right," the baron said. "There is no cause to pursue. We must hurry on. Time is against us. Forlorn awaits, and we must be there. We *must*."

"But, Baron, they tried to rob us once. They might—"

"They won't," Slocum said in a calm voice. "The shooting's over." He saw Maddy trembling, and he knew it wasn't from anxiety to be after the road agents. He wondered if she had ever shot a man before, much less killed one. From the wild-eyed look on her face, he doubted it.

"The circus is unprotected," she said, her voice shrill.

"Oh? You call what we did to those outlaws nothing?"

"No, I mean, oh—" She bit off the rest of her protest and turned away from Baron Fenstermacher. Slocum saw tears glistening on the woman's cheeks, leaving muddy tracks as they rolled down over dusty flesh.

"Let's you and me ride on ahead and be sure," Slocum suggested. Maddy jumped at the chance to hide her upset. She nodded curtly and put the spurs to her stallion. The powerful horse almost exploded as it raced away from the wagons.

"Keep the circus moving," Slocum told the baron, "and we'll keep the route ahead clear. I don't think anyone will sneak up on us from behind." He had been watching all day and saw no trace of anyone in back of them along the desolate road. The road agents had come at them from the north, from the rugged high country where he hadn't been able to get a decent view. Slocum raced away from the circus, catching up with Maddy a mile down the road.

"You all right?" he asked.

"No," she said, still crying. "I killed a man. I shot him, and I killed him!"

Slocum didn't bother telling her she'd killed more than one. He did say, "You saved my life. I was reloading, and he was getting ready to shoot me. And you definitely saved the baron and the others. I heard their leader say he wanted to kill the elephant himself."

She shuddered and hugged herself. The fringe on her vest moved like autumn's aspen leaves in a high wind. Her lips silently moved as she said to herself, "I killed him. I killed him."

"Maddy," Slocum said softly, "it was necessary. It was self-defense, them or us. Would you rather be buzzard bait? Would you rather see all the animals killed?"

"Of course not, but there must have been a better way. I'm a sharpshooter. I could have shot the gun from his hands."

Slocum's harsh laugh snapped her out of her fantasy. "There was no way you could ever do that. The distance was too great. It was one fine piece of shooting to hit a man-sized target, much less a tiny one like his hand."

"John, I promised never to hurt anyone."

"Who'd you promise?"

Madeleine Scowcroft looked back down the road in the direction of the wagons. "Let's get off the road, just for a while."

He saw she needed to talk. He urged his sorrel down a steep slope and then followed the arroyo uphill for a half mile until they came to a secluded area with a small spring bubbling up from the earth's depths. Slocum's horse was almost uncontrollable as it headed for the water. He dismounted and checked the water first, to make sure it wasn't laden with sulfur like so many springs in the mountains. It tasted pure and sweet and went down his throat like the finest whiskey he'd ever sampled.

He let his horse drink until Maddy rode into the cul de sac. Her horse drank sparingly, then they tethered their mounts some distance away to keep them from drinking themselves into a bloat. Slocum sat on the edge of the small pool, splashed water on his face and pulled his boots off to stick his feet into the water. Relief flowed through him. When he looked up he saw that Maddy had done the same thing.

"Who was it you promised?" he asked.

"My husband. Joseph said to never turn my rifle on anyone."

"Would he want you to die because you didn't? Would he want friends to die?"

"No, I reckon not," she said, her face drawn. "I miss him so."

"Where is he?"

"Dead," she said. "Tuberculosis. He taught me so much."

"How to shoot? He must have been a real marksman."

She shook her head, black hair slipping free and flying in all directions. She bent over and splashed water on her face. At this angle, Slocum couldn't help noticing that her vest had come open to reveal firm white breasts. He took a deep breath and tried to control his thoughts.

"He wasn't as good as I am. I've practiced constantly."

"You're good," Slocum said.

She looked up and her dark eyes were limpid. She said nothing as she stood. She unfastened the front of her vest and cast it aside, standing naked to the waist in the soft twilight. Shadows played across her face and chest, putting the lie to Slocum's notion that nothing could make her even more lovely. Maddy moved toward him, working at her tight-fitting britches, wiggling and turning, slipping free of them to stand naked above him.

"It's been so long for me, John. Don't deny me. Please." She reached out.

"Since your husband died?" he asked in surprise. She nodded mutely. "Why me?"

"You're so like him, John, so strong and sure. You even look a little like him. Oh, not in height or weight—Joseph was shorter and weighed almost nothing—but your eyes. They're the same color green as his."

She knelt down when he didn't make a move. Slocum was afraid she was a mirage and any motion would cause her to vanish. Maddy reached out and placed her hand on his crotch. Strong fingers began to massage, to knead, to work on the hardening length inside his trousers.

"I'm getting mighty uncomfortable," he said.

"If it's tight in there, then let's see about loosening it." She worked at his gunbelt and finally unbuckled it. Then Maddy ran her fingers under his trousers and began unbuttoning the fly. His erect organ leaped out. Slocum almost sighed in relief. It *had* been tight inside.

He gasped as she took the bulbous tip into her mouth and began tonguing it. Slocum leaned back on cool rock, his feet still in the pool. He stared up into the pink-tinted sunset clouds and reveled in the sensations rippling through his body—and they all started at the tip of Maddy's tongue. He struggled for a moment to get off his shirt. Somehow, without taking her mouth from him, Maddy skinned him from his pants.

"That feels good, but isn't there something more you'd like?" he asked. Slocum reached out and took her in his arms, pulling her down strongly. Her breasts crushed against his chest as their lips met in a passionate kiss. Time swung in crazy circles around them, speeding up with their pulses and yet seeming to stand still as they explored each other's bodies.

Slocum's hand ran across the woman's luxurious black hair, down her back, and finally stopped for a moment to cup her solid buttocks and pull her to him even harder. Maddy wiggled and giggled like a young girl and pushed up to look into his face.

"That tickles," she said. "Don't stop."

"Tickles? Rubbing your butt tickles? What does this do?" Slocum moved his hand even lower, through the fleshy crevice of her fleshy moons and found the area between her legs. Maddy stiffened with joy as his fingers rubbed across her most delicate flesh.

"Heaven," she moaned. "It's been so long. Too long."

"Are you saying this is too long?" Slocum pulled his hand back from its cramped position and worked it between them, stroking her slightly domed belly and then finding the tangle of pubic mat between her legs. He found the oily crevice, dipped briefly into it, and then gripped his own length and used this to torment her.

"Never, never, John," she sobbed out. She lay atop him, her legs drifting apart to open more fully for him. Slocum shifted his hips on the wet rock under him and then felt dampness against the purpled tip of his manhood. He arched his back and sank balls deep into the woman's yearning interior.

Maddy cried out as he plunged full length into her. His arms circled her and held her in place as they rolled over, Slocum now on top and between her legs. Maddy lifted those fine, long white legs on either side, bending them at the knees. Slocum sank even deeper into her heated cavity. For a moment he held himself back as he relished the feel of soft female flesh all around him. Then he couldn't restrain himself any longer.

His hips began moving, slowly at first and then with a life of their own. Friction mounted along his stiffness and spread throughout his loins. Maddy bucked and moaned under him, her body rising up to meet his every inward thrust.

"More, John, I need more of you. Harder! Tear me apart!" Her fingers clawed at his back and spurred him on.

Gasping, sweat pouring from his body, Slocum sped up even more until he found the proper depth and rhythm for their lovemaking. Maddy was babbling incoherently, and his own senses were jumbled.

He might have made love to a prettier woman but he couldn't remember when or where. Slocum felt the tightness in his groin turn to lava as he erupted into her. Maddy gasped and stiffened, then began moving frantically under him, lifting her buttocks off the ground and trying to take even more of his spewing organ into her body.

"Yes, oh, yes, I had forgotten what it's like. Keep moving, keep going, keep going;" she moaned over and over.

Slocum would have kept up the pace all day but his body had betrayed him with the burst of pleasure that had raced through him. All too soon he was no longer able to give her the delight he had even a few minutes earlier.

"Sorry, Maddy," he said, slumping down on top of her. The tight hard points of her nipples poked into his chest and told of her continued need. "You wore me out too fast. You're one hell of a woman."

"I'll take that as a compliment," she said, eyes closed and

an almost shy smile on her face. The eyes opened and fixed on his. "And I'll also take it as a challenge. I'd forgotten what I'd been missing."

Her hands moved over his body, touching all the right places. The next time he lasted longer, and both were satisfied at the outcome.

5

Cold wind with more than a hint of rain in it swept down from the high mountains. For Slocum it was a relief from the heat and dust he had endured for well nigh a week, but Maddy found it too cold for comfort. They had lain side by side on his saddle blanket for more than an hour after making love, and the sun had finally dipped behind the mountains. She shivered and pulled more of the blanket around her.

"Might be time we thought on getting back to the wagons," Slocum suggested.

"I wish I could lie here forever," she said, venting a deep sigh. "I'm not lying. It has been a long time for me. When Joseph died, I didn't know what to do. Shooting became my life. It was as if I could be the best at what he'd taught me, a part of him wouldn't die."

"As long as you remember, he won't die," Slocum said, somewhat uncomfortable. He felt as if he wasn't sidled up next to the naked woman as much as a memory was. He had found that he could compete with another man on just about any terms and come out ahead, but there was no way he could win against the memory of a lost husband.

"I reckon so," she said, sitting up. She had all the blanket now, and Slocum had to go reaching for his shirt and pants to shield himself against the wind. "The baron's good to me, and the others are about all the friends I have in the world. But I do miss Joseph." She snuggled closer, and Slocum wondered what he was getting himself into with her. Madeleine Scowcroft was a powerful pretty lady, but the way she talked sounded as if she was husband hunting.

Slocum finished dressing as he turned over the possibilities in his head. He wasn't the settling down kind. The run-in he'd had with that carpetbagger judge back in Georgia had made sure of that, but Maddy wasn't exactly the stay-at-home sort, either. No one who pulled up stakes and moved on every few days to work with the circus could be considered a homebody. And she used that Winchester as good as any man Slocum had ever seen—and he had seen some of the best there were.

"The circus looks to be in trouble," Slocum said carefully. "Have you given any thought to what you'd do if the baron was forced to quit touring?"

"The money problems have always haunted us," she said, beginning to get into her clothing. Watching as she squeezed into her tight britches was a pleasure that almost matched what they had finished doing. She moved this way and that and everything wiggled just right. She slipped into her fringed vest and began lacing it up the front, leaving her tanned arms bare and covered with gooseflesh from the increasingly cold wind whipping off the mountains.

Slocum had seen wind like this before, and it always meant a storm was brewing.

"There wasn't a whole lot of money made back in town," Slocum said, still trying to remember the name of the Utah city they'd been in. From the look of the country, Forlorn, Utah, was a good name for the one they were heading toward.

"No, thanks to Clay Wilkins," she said bitterly. Maddy picked up her rifle and checked the magazine, as if she'd be using it right away on the Bogardus Shooting Team member. "The baron might be riding on ahead to be sure that the baggage will arrive about the same time the animals do. It's best if we get back and see if we're needed." There was a hint of sadness in her voice. Slocum could live with her feeling guilty about betraying the memory of her dead husband, but he wouldn't stand still for the woman accusing him of taking advantage of her grieving. She had wanted what they'd done as much as he had.

Slocum got their horses ready and helped Maddy up on her stallion. The powerful horse snorted and pawed at the ground, ready to run. Slocum's sorrel was less enthusiastic about having its rider's weight on its back again. Slocum patted the animal's neck to let it know he appreciated loyalty.

They rode back to the road and saw that the wagons had passed by some time earlier. Slocum hadn't realized they'd been so long back in the rocks. The time had passed quickly and pleasurably. He studied the way the dirt had been disturbed, made an estimate of how long the brisk wind had been blowing and said, "They're about an hour ahead of us. We ought to catch them before the storm hits."

Maddy looked up at the tall peaks and nodded. She pulled down the brim of her huge hat and bent forward, urging on her white stallion. The horse trotted off. Slocum followed, alert for any trouble other than the weather that might be brewing. As far as he could tell, the circus wagons were all that had come this way for a long spell. Of the road agents he saw not a trace.

Maddy kept ahead of him, not wanting to talk. This was all right by Slocum since he wasn't as distracted from watching for spoor along the road, but he found himself looking at her trim figure from time to time until the night closed in and left them in almost complete dark until the moon rose.

And then she glowed like an angel. Her dark hair bannered away from her face as they rode into the increasingly sharp wind. The fringe on her vest snapped like miniature whips, and he saw her shivering, bare arms exposed to the wind's bite.

"Here," he said, riding up beside her and passing over his duster. "It'll keep you a tad warmer."

"Thanks, John," she said, hardly looking his way as she took the long canvas garment. She shrugged into it and fastened its front. Even in the shapeless duster, there was no mistaking that Madeleine Scowcroft was a lovely woman.

"There," she said suddenly. "Campfire. That must be where they stopped for the night."

Slocum couldn't argue. Her sharp eyes had spotted the small, dancing flames before he had, but he admitted to himself he had been distracted. As they got closer, Slocum saw there were a dozen or more of the cook fires. This was either one hell of a big outlaw band, or Maddy was right about it being the circus.

The animal handlers greeted them, being alerted to their arrival by the pacing of their caged wards. A toothless lion let out a weak roar, and Trajan trumpeted loud enough to wake the dead.

"You have been scouting for us?" came Morelli's voice. Slocum looked around and finally saw the wire-walker sitting beside a tiny cooking fire.

"Route's clear," Slocum said, wanting to give the impression that they had been hard at work rather than idling the time away. "The only trouble on the horizon is the storm."

"What storm?" Morelli asked. "Look at this sky. See the stars! They are so close I can reach up and touch them."

Slocum snorted and stared at the man. Finding poetry in the sky was one thing, ignoring the build-up of the storm clouds was another. Already the stars Morelli enthused over so much were vanishing under heavy rolls of rain cloud. Slocum dismounted and tethered his horse nearby; Maddy did the same.

"Where's the baron? Did he ride ahead?" Slocum asked.

"That he did," Morelli said. "He is looking to Forlorn to bail us out of our financial woes. He listens too much to Kincaid, if you ask me. Kincaid is no good for us."

Slocum snorted again, knowing there wasn't enough money in any small Utah town to keep Baron Fenstermacher's Fabulous Continental Circus afloat. With any luck they'd get their railroad cars back and not have to cross the rugged terrain to their next performance, wherever it might be. And no matter what happened, Slocum knew they'd find themselves competing directly with the Sells Brothers Circus—and Clay Wilkins's crew.

"What's for supper?" Slocum asked, his belly growling loudly. It had been too long since he'd eaten.

"We have a little," Morelli said. Before the small man could reach across and stir the beans in the black kettle sitting at the edge of the fire, lightning split the nighttime sky, dazzling them and causing a stir among the animals. Trajan bellowed and stamped his huge feet, and the other beasts began protesting the thunder that rolled across the camp like an inexorable tide.

"So close," muttered Morelli. "You were right about the storm. I apologize. I thought you were . . ." His voice trailed off, and he averted his eyes. Slocum glanced at Maddy and saw her blush. Morelli had been right on target with what he'd been thinking, and only the obvious had rescued the woman's reputation among her coworkers.

Heavy drops of cold water began splattering around them. Slocum went to his saddlebags and fished out a bright yellow slicker. To his surprise, the others in the camp weren't seeking dry spots for themselves. Most were trying to calm the animals and keep them from battering against the bars of their cages.

"Is there any danger?" Slocum asked Maddy. "With the animals?"

"I don't think so. The cages are sturdy, and this won't be the first time the animals have been wet. Neither Leo nor Simba—the lions—will like it, but it's nothing they haven't endured before."

The words were hardly out of her mouth when the elephant protested loudly. The rain started pouring from the sky, the pounding of drops against the rock and dirt momentarily drowning out the frightened beast's cries. Slocum pulled the slicker closer around him, hunted for a sheltered spot for his horse and found nothing. He had to satisfy himself with getting his gear stowed under a wagon.

"John, John!" he heard over the wind and rain. "Help! Help us!"

He tried to find Maddy in the downpour and couldn't. Cursing, he crawled out from under the sheltering wagon and was hit full blast in the face by the driving rain. Pulling his Stetson down to shield his face, he shouldered his way into the storm. Brilliant flashes of lightning showed the way to where the woman and two of the animal handlers huddled beside a large boulder.

As he got closer he saw that it wasn't a boulder but an overturned wagon. Slocum tried to remember what had been loaded onto this wagon but couldn't. If one of the big cats had escaped, there'd be hell to pay. A lion, even Leo the toothless monarch that the baron had bought in St. Louis, was twice the size of any predator in these mountains. Since it was out of its jungle and had no handler to feed it, the animal would fall easy prey to packs of wild dogs, coyotes, or even other prowling cats. A lean, young, hungry cougar was more than a match for an African lion used to the warmth of the veldt.

"What happened?"

"He got loose, John. We've got to track him down," Maddy said.

"One of the lions?"

"Trajan!"

Slocum went cold inside. Hunting down a lion wouldn't have been much different than finding a cougar—it would have been easier. But the elephant was dangerous because of its sheer size. Slocum didn't think he had anything heavy enough to bring down a rampaging elephant, either. Even a .69 Sharps buffalo gun might not be powerful enough to kill the mountain of bellowing flesh that was Trajan.

"Did the storm spook him?"

"No, it's not just that," Maddy said. She motioned for the elephant's handler to come over and explain.

"The elephant's in must," Andre said, wiping rain from his eyes. "The baron knows it's better to use females in a circus, but Trajan was cheap—and he's about the most impressive damned elephant I've ever seen."

"What are you talking about?" Slocum asked.

"He's sort of in heat," Maddy said. "Bull elephants go crazy when it's mating season."

"Trajan thinks *this* is mating season?" A new round of lightning lent eerie shadows to the landscape. Slocum jumped as thunder rolled past from higher in the mountains. What did a horny elephant sound like, and what would it do to a man trying to stop it?

"Dangerous," Andre said. "Damned dangerous. There's no way you can possibly shoot it. No rifle's that powerful. You'd only infuriate Trajan further."

"I wasn't planning on killing the elephant," Slocum said, lying. The fear of being trampled by the animal came and went. "How do we control it?"

The handler shook his head. "There's not much we can do until we find Trajan. Do we have to wait for the storm to let up? I've never seen it rain this hard."

"It's a real frog strangler," Slocum allowed. Sheets of driving water obscured any chance of seeing more than a few yards, yet he knew what he had to do. He pulled the slicker around him to keep it from flapping in the wind, lowered his head and then dashed out. He was a damn fool for bothering, he told himself, but he had taken the job with the baron's circus, and he wasn't the kind to shirk what he saw as his duty. The animal trainers knew their jobs. Maddy was a hell of a trick shot. Morelli walked on a tight wire and ate fire.

John Slocum tracked.

He tried to find any trace of the elephant's footprints, but the rain obscured the ground. He had to rely on some sixth sense to follow the frightened, horny animal through the storm. Slocum turned and twisted, went up draws, and avoided the deep, filled-to-flooding arroyos, remembering what Maddy had said about elephants not being able to jump over even shallow trenches.

Slocum found the elephant almost by accident. He thought he'd heard the wind moaning through trees higher up the slope; it was Trajan caught in a muddy mire. The way the beast thrashed around kept Slocum at bay. He studied the problem the best he could and saw the real problem. The more Trajan struggled, the deeper into the sucking mud he sank. The area must have been part of a mountain stream-fed pool for the ground to be this muddy before the rain came pouring down.

"What now?" came the question.

Slocum jumped at the sound of Maddy's voice. He had thought he was alone. Somehow, she had followed him as he tracked down the elephant.

"Damned if I know. We need to talk to the trainer."

"I brought ropes," Maddy said. "I can throw a lariat with the best." She handed a coil of hemp rope to him. Slocum took it and looked skeptically at the trumpeting elephant. Such a powerful animal could break a rope designed to do nothing more than bring down a calf.

"We'll need more than the pair of us," Slocum said. "But this is a start. We need to rope the elephant from several different directions and hogtie it until it calms down."

"Andre will be here in a few seconds," said Maddy.

Slocum made his way around the mire and climbed onto a rain-slippery rock. The first thing he looked for was a place to tie the rope after he roped Trajan. He found a good-sized pine tree that would do.

The storm pounding around him, Slocum stood on the rock, swinging the rope over his head. Trajan jerked his head back and forth, gray skin lost in the black of the night and rain. A vivid bolt of lightning lit the scene. Slocum acted without thinking. He loosed the rope, dropping the loop over Trajan's head.

The sudden jerk upon the rope almost pulled Slocum off the rock. He dropped to his knees and managed to swing around to brace himself with one foot. Fighting the frightened beast was out of the question. All Slocum intended to do was keep from ending up in the mire under the elephant's hooves. He was given a moment's respite when another lightning bolt showed a second rope arcing up and over Trajan. Slocum used the distraction to get his end of the rope around the tree trunk. He secured it just as Trajan tugged on the rope.

The tree groaned and was almost uprooted. Slocum didn't stand and watch. He was making his way around the fighting beast to join Maddy. She fought to get the free end of her rope around a rock. It took both of them to secure it. Slocum sat back and saw that only two ropes would never hold Trajan.

"More," he shouted over the rain, "we need more ropes."

"Here. Here are more, but I do not know what to do with them." Andre staggered up against the wind with a half dozen more lariats. Where he had found them, Slocum didn't know or care. He grabbed one, fought to get it untangled from the others, then swung it, and dropped the loop over the elephant after the third try. This rope he secured to a tree some distance away from the others.

Maddy tried to help with another toss but missed repeatedly. Slocum worked his way around Trajan until the elephant was secured like a spider in the center of a hemp web.

"Good, very good," Andre finally said. "Not even an elephant as large as Trajan can break free from that."

Slocum sank down, back to a rock, and let the rain pour across his face. He was exhausted from the struggle to secure Trajan, but he had won. There wasn't anything else that could possibly go wrong, and for that Slocum was thankful.

6

Trajan exhausted himself an hour after the downpour slowed to a drizzle. Slocum, Maddy, and Andre watched the elephant finally sink into the mire and stop fighting against the dozen ropes lassoing him. For this respite Slocum was glad. The trees they'd used as anchors were beginning to pull out of the rain-soaked ground. If Trajan had continued to fight his imprisonment, he would have broken free. Hunting down a rogue elephant was the last thing Slocum wanted to do. He was so tired he could hardly keep his eyes open.

He jumped when he felt something moving against his side. He had been dozing off, and Maddy had come up, laying her head against his shoulder. He settled back uncomfortably, wondering if Andre was the gossiping sort. Besmirching Maddy's reputation with the people she valued so highly wasn't anything Slocum wanted to do.

He wondered how he got himself into such fixes. Wet-nursing an elephant half again as tall as he was seemed like the most damnfool thing in the world. He turned slightly as Maddy snuggled closer into the curve of his arm and let out a contented little sigh. He stared at her and thought of the hours they'd spent off the trail. It might have been years ago, but Slocum knew it was less than twelve hours in the past. He wasn't sure what he felt about Maddy, and he was confused as hell about what she thought of him. He refused to be a substitute for her dead husband, but there had seemed to be something more. Now and then.

He just didn't know.

He was drifting off to sleep again when Trajan bellowed. Andre began shouting in some foreign language that might have been French, and Maddy jerked upright, startled awake.

"What's wrong?" she asked.

Andre was beside himself. "The elephant is going to strangle. There are too many ropes. See how they cut into his neck?"

Slocum saw the problem right away. The elephant was sinking deeper into the mire. Slocum raced to the nearest rope and cut it free, using the thick-bladed knife he carried sheathed at the small of his back. He didn't stop, but hacked at the next rope and the next and the next. He paused and saw that Maddy and Andre had each succeeded in getting ropes free. Four lariats still held Trajan in place.

"Let's get him out," Slocum called. "Has he calmed down enough for that?"

"Let us pray that this is so," Andre said, crossing himself. Slocum ignored both the animal trainer and Maddy as he edged around to face the elephant. Trajan's eyes were white-rimmed. In a horse this meant panic. Slocum saw no reason to think it meant anything different in the trapped, gray-skinned behemoth. Slocum had plenty of experience wrangling to know what had to be done.

Whooping and hollering like a renegade Indian, Slocum got the elephant's attention. He then used a short length of rope to swat the elephant's head, causing it to surge back and forth and give it direction for escaping the bog. Tugging on ropes on either side, Maddy and Andre kept Trajan's head turned toward Slocum. Inch by agonizing inch, Slocum lured the elephant from the sticky mire. He marvelled at how deep the mud had gone and the powerful suction holding the animal down. The lewd sucking noise echoing down the mountain slopes told Slocum the elephant had pulled free.

Trajan shook himself and then trumpeted in joy, using his trunk to throw mud everywhere. Andre hurried to the elephant's side and used a hook on a long pole to examine the neck and underside.

"He is well," Andre said. "The must is not possessing him now. It is safe to get him back to the camp."

Andre patted Trajan's head, and the elephant hoisted his trainer to a perch just behind his large flapping ears. Slocum and Maddy made their way down the mountain, letting the now gentle rain wash away mud as they walked in silence. Andre guided Trajan behind them until they reached the circus camp.

Slocum shook his slicker clear of water, peered at the slowly brightening sky, and realized he hadn't gotten any sleep to speak of during the night. The storm had passed but his tiredness only increased. He yawned widely and went to get his gear under the wagon. Already, the men responsible for the wagon were getting it ready to roll. There wouldn't be any rest for any of them today.

"We've got to keep a good pace if we want to get to Forlorn by this evening," Maddy told him. She looked at him for a moment, then smiled almost sadly. "You look beat. Why don't you try sleeping a spell and then catch up later with the wagons?"

He studied her for any sign that she was half as tired as he was. She had been through everything he had, yet Maddy gave no sign that she was the least bit tuckered out. If anything, she seemed to feel pity for him that he was bushed.

"I can get on with the wagons," he said. He had gone longer without sleep, and he had the feeling that Baron Fenstermacher was riding into trouble at Forlorn—and so was Maddy.

"I'm glad," she said, giving him a faint smile. Slocum wasn't able to figure out what was going on with the woman. She seemed to want him around, and yet there was a distance between them that had developed after they'd made love. Maddy turned and began shouting orders. The others obeyed. Slocum figured she was the head wrangler when the baron wasn't around.

He saddled his horse and rode up and down examining the wagons, garnering a few half-hearted growls from the big cats and a joyously loud trumpet from Trajan. Andre waved to him from the perch high atop the elephant. Slocum touched the brim of his hat in acknowledgment and rode to the rear of the small wagon train. Everything was in order for another day's travel.

At the front of the line of wagons, Maddy waved her arm to signal an advance, fringed sleeve flapping in a new day's breeze. Slowly the wagons rumbled off, Slocum bringing up the rear. It was going to be a long, hard ride.

Forlorn, Utah, lived up to its name. Seldom had Slocum seen a more desolate place. The wind whipped down through the mountain passes and turned the city streets as frigid as winter. He almost expected snow flurries to dust the buildings with a thin coating of frost, but it was too late in the year for real snow. In spite of the weather, the entire population of the town must have turned out to see the baron's wagons come rolling in.

Slocum counted no fewer than a hundred people—but he saw the freight cars on a railroad siding emblazoned with the Sells Brothers Circus banners. The other circus had already come to town and might have upstaged the baron again.

Slocum smiled slightly at the obvious enthusiasm from the men, women, and children watching the miniature parade. The baron and a few of the baggage handlers worked through the crowd passing out flyers. This was the first taste he'd had of fame, though it was diffused among all the circus performers. He found himself uncomfortable at even the smallest bit of attention, though. Too many Wanted posters drifted through the West with his name and likeness on them. The law never forgot judge killers, and here he was putting himself at the center of attention. Slocum dropped back a few yards and rode alongside Trajan. This gave him instant anonymity. Even the most jaded would stare up at the nine-foot-tall elephant with a hint of awe.

Baron Fenstermacher shouted from the top of a rain barrel rolled over to give him a stage, "Gather around in an hour, ladies and gentleman, and see the best parade ever! I give you Baron Fenstermacher's Fabulous Continental Circus!" The baron jumped down and started passing out his broadsides once more.

Maddy guided the wagons into place alongside those still laden with the huge circus tent and other gear. Now that the full complement was present, they could begin erecting the big top and seeing to other preparations for the evening performance. Slocum heaved a sigh of exhaustion. They had ridden two days straight, endured heavy storms and road agents and Trajan getting stuck in mud, and they weren't even going to rest.

"The show must go on," Maddy said.

"Reckon so," Slocum allowed. "What's the flyer say? The baron surely got it printed up fast enough."

Maddy held one of the baron's advertisements. The expression on her face told Slocum something was wrong. She silently handed it to him. He read it quickly, then looked up at her.

"I don't understand why he's wasting so much space telling what sonsabitches they are in the other circus, even if it is true."

"That's a rat bill," she said. "The baron had said he'd never distribute them. The idea is to badmouth other acts and make your own sound bigger, better, more grand. This must be Kincaid's idea. The baron is too decent to resort to such a thing."

"Does he have to do it to get an audience?" Slocum looked over to where Andre and another handler worked getting the trail dust off Trajan. "That monster alone ought to pack in the crowds. I've never seen a beast that big."

Maddy laughed and said, "You think that because you had to pull Trajan out of the bog. The Sells Brothers's Jumbo is a sight all by herself. And their other animals are better than ours."

Slocum wondered if he ought to tell Maddy what he knew about Wilkins sending their railroad cars on, forcing them to make the two day trip across country. He held back. This would only throw fuel onto a fire that might be better off dying down.

"You!" came the loud shout. "You did this!"

Slocum glanced over his shoulder and saw Clay Wilkins storming up, angrily waving one of the baron's handbills. "You can't tell all these lies and get away with it."

Slocum turned back to Maddy, his hand going to his six-shooter and slipping the leather thong off the hammer. He said, "There's going to be a bit of trouble. Don't get involved."

"But John—" She stepped back and her eyes widened. This was all the warning Slocum needed. He ducked, spun and sent his fist out to land squarely in the pit of Wilkins's belly.

The man grunted and stumbled back, his face bright red. He caught his breath and let out a roar. He charged, arms flailing wildly. Slocum saw Wilkins wasn't much of a fighter, at least when it came to fist fighting. He ducked under a wild punch and drove another short left into the man's midsection. The jolt passed all the way up into Slocum's shoulder. It was like hitting a pine board, but Wilkins reeled under the shock.

Slocum saw that Wilkins wasn't armed. If he had been, Slocum wouldn't have hesitated going for his Colt Navy. As it was, Wilkins seemed to want to do nothing but absorb the punishment Slocum was so willingly giving him. He came at Slocum again and again took a heavy punch to the chest. Slocum knew better than to hit a man in the jaw. It might knock out his opponent but was more likely to inflict serious damage on the bones in his hand.

A loud cry from Baron Fenstermacher's roustabouts went up as Wilkins came at Slocum again. A half dozen men crowded in close, pushing, shoving, punching, and Slocum found himself caught up in the middle of a free-for-all. He tried to find Wilkins in the melee but couldn't. All the men fighting near him were the baron's workers. The fight expanded like water spilled on a floor, starting in the middle and rapidly pouring out.

Slocum dodged a flying fist and found himself crashing into Maddy. They went down on the ground in a jumble of arms and legs. He struggled to get up and only made matters worse. They tumbled back to the ground wrapped around each other.

"It's not that this isn't interesting," Slocum said, "but I want Wilkins right now."

"I saw him trying to run, the yellow-bellied coward!" She rolled and came to her feet in a lithe movement. Slocum was slower in getting up but still managed to catch her arm and swing her around as she tried to rush after Wilkins.

"This isn't your fight," Slocum said.

"It is, too!"

Slocum held on and kept her from plunging back into the fight. He had seen what was going on. The town sheriff and four deputies had arrived and were going through the worst of the fight, plucking out the baron's men. The sheriff got to Slocum and Maddy, who were just standing and watching.

The sheriff's gaze dropped to the well-worn ebony handle of Slocum's Colt and then slowly worked back up to the cold green eyes. "You ain't takin' part in this fight, are you?"

"Sheriff," cried Maddy, "Clay Wilkins started the fight. He—"

Slocum silenced her with pressure on her arm.

"It's all just a friendly misunderstanding," he said. "There's no need to get all hot and bothered over it." Slocum looked past the bandy-legged, truculent little sheriff and knew a big deal was being made of it. The deputies were as happy as hogs in garbage arresting the baron's men. A few of the townspeople had joined in just for the fun of a good fight. They were being sent on their way, and the few men who didn't belong had to be from the Sells Brothers Circus.

"That ain't the way I see it," the sheriff said, spitting and hitting the toe of Slocum's boot. "Got to keep the peace or you drifters will try walkin' all over us local folks."

Slocum kept Maddy from telling the sheriff off. He knew it wouldn't do any good.

Clay Wilkins had set them up by starting a fight over the rat bill, and the town sheriff had ended it. At least a half dozen of the baron's men were going to be spending the night in jail. Slocum hoped enough were on the right side of the iron bars to put on a decent performance.

7

"You've got to stop them!" Maddy cried. She struggled in Slocum's grip, but he held on firmly. If he let her go, there'd be hell to pay—and she'd end up in the town lockup just like a dozen others of the baron's crew.

"Cool down," he said. "This isn't any accident or mistake. Wilkins planned it. Unless I miss my guess, he's paid off that bandy-legged, cantankerous sheriff. Nothing you say is going to have any effect, unless you offer him more of a bribe."

"But the men being arrested are performers!"

Slocum had noticed that, too. In spite of all the roustabouts entering the fray, the deputies had singled out the men who actually performed. A trick rider, two trapeze artists, and three of the circus clowns had been dragged off to jail. Wilkins had crippled the circus with those arrests, but there were still enough performers left to put on a decent show.

Then Slocum saw Andre being dragged through the streets, shouting incoherently in his own language. Anger welled inside but Slocum swallowed it. He wouldn't do the men any good getting thrown into a cell alongside them. If anything, for Slocum it might mean a long jail sentence. Or a stretched neck. All it took was the sheriff remembering a

Wanted poster, and Slocum would be hanged and left for a buzzard's breakfast.

"He didn't do anything!" Maddy cried. Slocum hung on grimly.

"Wilkins wants you to make a fuss," he said. "We've got to be cleverer than he is." He scanned the crowd and saw the hatchet-faced sharpshooter standing nearby, arms crossed and a smirk on his lips. It shouldn't be too hard to outsmart a man like this, but Wilkins had gotten the upper hand twice. Slocum didn't want to look foolish a third time, even if Maddy and the baron didn't know what he did about the missed railroad cars.

"He's innocent! He didn't do anything!"

"Lady, you want to do some time with them?" asked the sheriff. "I can't abide by a shrill female, and you're hurtin' my eardrums with your caterwauling."

"It's all right, Sheriff," Slocum said, whirling Maddy around so she was almost thrown toward the circus tent. "She gets this way sometimes. You know how it is with high-strung women."

The sheriff spat again, again hitting Slocum's boots. The man waited a few seconds to see if Slocum reacted. When he didn't, the lawman spun and waddled off, his legs bowing outward slightly as he hurried toward his jail to see what the bogus fight had brought his way.

"That son of a bitch!" stormed Maddy. "Why'd you let him get by with it?"

"No way to fight him now, but there'll be a way later. We've got to bide our time and see." Slocum paused and wondered who Maddy meant. She was glaring at the sheriff as if it was all his fault. Clay Wilkins laughed and sauntered toward a small café down the street, his dirty work done for the time.

"Wilkins has it in for you and the baron, doesn't he?"

"It's as much Bogardus as Wilkins," she said. "I can beat Wilkins, and I know I can beat Captain Bogardus, given the chance."

"Cracked balls," Slocum muttered. Subterfuge was required, not brute force. Bogardus was a master at being sneaky. Slocum saw no reason to let him keep a monopoly on it.

"What are you talking about? We've got to get them out."

"Let's go talk to the sheriff," Slocum said, "but I don't want you to let out so much as a peep, no matter what he says or does. He's in cahoots with Wilkins and is looking for an excuse to put the baron's biggest-drawing act in jail."

"Me?"

Slocum had to laugh at her. For a beautiful, talented woman she was singularly free of vanity.

"You're the only reason I'd come to see the baron's show twice," Slocum said. "The elephant is impressive, but only once. You are memorable, you riding that white stallion of yours."

Maddy blushed and tried to keep from looking like a schoolgirl being kissed for the first time. She didn't entirely succeed.

"We'll see what the sheriff wants to let them out of jail, but I'll wager there's not that kind of money among everyone in the circus."

They hurried to the jailhouse, passing the café where Wilkins had started chowing down on a meal big enough for an elephant. Slocum kept walking. The time would come when he and Wilkins had it out, but it would have to be later after the baron got his performers back for the evening show.

The sheriff looked up from an almost bare desk. Wanted posters had been used to stuff the cracks in the walls, keeping out the cold wind. Slocum doubted anyone in Forlorn bothered much to look at the posters they got from the federal marshal.

"What do you two want?" the sheriff demanded in his truculent manner. Slocum kept the desk between him and lawman to prevent a sudden gob from hitting him. The sheriff looked disappointed when he saw that Slocum wasn't in position, turned, and accurately hit a brass spittoon with a loud *ping!*

"We're here to apologize for our men, Sheriff," Slocum said. "We've been out on the road for a spell, and they went a bit wild when they hit town. Blowing off a little steam shouldn't be a crime, especially since it won't happen again."

Slocum grabbed Maddy by the arm and squeezed hard when she started to protest. He wished he had left her back at the circus. One mistake now, and she'd land in a cell for sure.

"An apology now? That's why you're wasting my time?"

"What else can we do, Sheriff?" Slocum asked, waiting for the amount of the bribe the lawman was going to ask to spring the dozen circus performers.

"We got disturbin' the peace charges against them. Now that's a night in jail or a hundred-dollar fine. You willin' to pay the fine and get 'em out?"

"A hundred dollars apiece?" Maddy staggered backward, trembling with anger.

"Too rich for our blood, Sheriff. Reckon they'd better serve their time," Slocum said quickly, wanting to get the woman out before the lawman found a reason to keep them overnight, too. He steered Maddy into the street before releasing his grip on her elbow.

"That's robbery, John! He's extorting us. The baron can't pay over a thousand dollars. Maybe we can get one or two out, but even then, even a hundred dollars is more than we're likely to raise."

"Don't worry on that score," Slocum said. "The sheriff's not going to let just one out, even if you happen to come up with the fine. Wilkins has him in his hip pocket, and the sheriff's not going to budge unless we up the ante."

"We can't do it. We'll have to cancel the evening performance. The baron won't do a show unless it's the best he can deliver."

"Let's walk a spell," Slocum said.

"John, really. We have to tell the baron, not that he probably doesn't already know. Bad news travels fast."

Slocum walked up and down the street with Maddy muttering beside him. He didn't pay a whole lot of attention to her because he was too busy studying the jail. He had seen more secure ones in his day, but breaking the performers out wasn't exactly what he had in mind. The sheriff would relish nothing more than coming after them. Wilkins might even pay a bonus if the lawman could send a few of them to the territorial prison.

"I've seen enough," Slocum said. "I need to talk some things over with the baron and a few of the others."

"You're not going to break them out, are you?"

Slocum wondered at how her mind worked. She knew the men in the tiny cells weren't guilty of anything but working for Baron Fenstermacher, and yet Maddy wanted to obey the letter of the law. When he got down to trying to save the baron's circus, though, he knew she wouldn't hold back.

"Even better than breaking them out," Slocum assured her. "Go get the baron and have him bring a dozen men he can trust—just roustabouts, not performers," Slocum said. He thought hard and added, "And don't breathe a word of this to Kincaid, either."

Maddy looked at him curiously, then went to obey. Slocum stood just inside the big top. The tent was ominously empty and dark, a hint of what would happen unless Andre and the others were on hand in a few hours for the performance. The Sells Brothers Circus had the upper hand with its exotic variety of animals, but Slocum knew the baron's circus could hold its own, given the chance.

"What a disaster!" declared Baron Fenstermacher, storming into the tent with Maddy and the others trailing like ducklings trying to keep up with their mother.

"I've got a plan, Baron," Slocum said, "but it'll be risky for some of your men."

"We need Andre to handle Trajan," moaned the baron, stroking his mustache. "Without the big elephant, there is no show." He turned and put his hand on Maddy's shoulder, correcting himself. "I did not mean to say they will not come for the sharpshooter act, my dear. But the big elephant, that is the circus."

"How many of the men in jail do you really need to carry off the performance?" Slocum listened as the men discussed the matter. The baron held up his hand and said, "Andre, of course. Three others." He named them. "So what will you do?"

"Leave that part to me, Baron," Slocum said. "You get ready for the performance. I'll have Andre and the other three here in time. I promise." As he spoke he was aware of Maddy watching him closely. She took a step closer before she spoke.

"John, how can I help?"

"Get ready for the show," he told her. "I don't want you locked up if this doesn't work." She started to argue but the baron spoke quickly to her. She chewed her lower lip and then finally agreed to set up her targets for the performance. With some reluctance Slocum watched her go since he trusted her more than he did the others with him.

"So?" asked the baron. "What is it that must be done?"

"You don't want to know," Slocum said. He chased the baron off and then spoke earnestly with the roustabouts. It took a few minutes to convince them his scheme would work before four volunteered. Slocum wasted no time starting off for the jail once he had worked out the details of his scheme.

He waited impatiently until a minor ruckus started in the café, leaving only a single deputy inside the jail. The sheriff and another deputy hustled out and quickly vanished into the restaurant. Slocum signaled two of the burly circus workers. They positioned themselves in front of the door to the jail and began to fight, shouting and cursing so that only the dead or deaf could have ignored them.

The solitary deputy left in the jail came out to see what was happening and immediately found himself caught up in the fight.

"Break it up, you two. I don't want no fightin' in front of the damn jail! It's not seemly." The deputy looked uneasy at the notion that the sheriff might return and find the disturbance on his own doorstep. "Get on along now, you hear?"

The men continued to fight and finally both turned and wrestled the deputy to the ground, sandwiching him between their flailing arms and kicking feet. It was time for the next part of the plan. Slocum and four others edged along the wall of the jail and then ducked into the office. Slocum rummaged through the deputy's desk and found the keys to the cells in the rear of the building.

"Slocum!" called Andre when he saw who was coming into the cell block. "You are breaking us out!"

"Not exactly. Get out, you and you and you two," Slocum said, pointing out the performers. "The rest of you are going to have to spend the night as guests of the town of Forlorn."

Protests went up and then confusion settled in when the four who had accompanied Slocum entered the cells to take the place of the performers. Andre saw immediately what Slocum had in mind and helped make the switch.

"We will do the show tonight, eh?" Andre asked, chuckling.

"Not if you don't shake your ass and get out of here." Slocum heard the deputy shouting for help. If the sheriff returned now, they might all get caught. The baron would have nineteen men in jail then and have to call off both performance and moving on until the men were free.

Andre and the other three rushed from the jailhouse and into the street. Slocum followed and saw the danger coming down the street. Not only was the sheriff returning, he had two deputies with him. Slocum dived into the fight and pulled the men apart.

"Are you crazy?" he yelled. "You want to spend the night in jail for disturbing the peace, like the others?" He cast a quick glance at Andre, who lowered his face and partially hid it in shadows formed by flickering gas lights at the end of the street.

"You go on now and stop this fightin'," the sheriff said. He pushed through the small crowd, never noticing that it was comprised of men who'd just escaped from his jail. "Tell me what's going on, Josiah."

"Sheriff, they was fighting to beat the band, and I tried to break it up. They was—"

"Check the prisoners," he snapped to a deputy at his side. The other deputy drew his six-shooter and covered the crowd. Slocum held his breath until the deputy in the jailhouse had made his superficial examination of the prisoners.

"We still got 'em all, Sheriff," he called.

"You boys get on out of here or I *will* throw you in the clink. I don't like no disturbance in Forlorn."

Slocum held out his arms and rounded up the men, herding them toward the edge of town where the huge circus tent flapped in the wind. He held off letting out a whoop of glee until he got inside the tent.

"You give the show of your lives," he told the performers. Andre came over and stared at Slocum, then solemnly held out his hand. Slocum shook it. Andre grinned broadly and rushed off to get Trajan ready for the evening's performance.

In less than an hour, Baron Fenstermacher began his spiel, and in ninety minutes the tent had filled with curious townspeople. Slocum wasn't sure if the baron was making any money or if this was a free performance, but the crowd responded well to the opening acts, one by a man who'd been in the Forlorn jail two hours earlier, and they roared with laughter as the two clowns cavorted and cajoled.

But the audience went wild when Maddy came riding in and did her act. Slocum marveled again at how good a marksman the woman was. She made her last shot, breaking two clay pipes with a single bullet, then stood in the stirrups and took a well-deserved ovation. As she rode past, she smiled at him.

If the crowd had responded well to Maddy, they were even more appreciative of Trajan. Andre's handling of the massive beast was masterful, and no one else could have done half the job he did. But Slocum's attention drifted to the entrance and a dark figure standing there watching everything inside.

Slocum dropped down and rolled under the canvas, coming to his feet outside. He hadn't thought it was hot inside the tent until he felt the cold wind whipping past his face. It took him a few seconds for his vision to adjust to the dark, but when it did Slocum turned even colder inside.

Clay Wilkins had been watching the performance and was on his way to tell the sheriff that his prisoners had escaped—and Slocum saw no way of reaching him to stop him.

8

Slocum considered shooting Clay Wilkins in the back, then decided the man was too far away in the dark for an accurate shot. But if he didn't stop Wilkins, the sheriff would know a switch had somehow been made and throw the baron and everyone else into the clink. Slocum couldn't overtake Wilkins on foot, but there was a faster way to cut the man off from his goal.

Slocum ran to his horse and vaulted into the saddle. Even as he swung the sorrel's head around, he was reaching for the lariat looped on the leather thong near the saddlehorn. The rope still smelled of elephant, but Slocum found that appropriate. The horse exploded forward at a full gallop. Slocum's legs tightened on the horse's flanks and he leaned forward to make a good toss.

Wilkins heard the pounding hooves and turned around to see what was going on.

His eyes widened in surprise when he saw the lariat dropping down over him, but all he could do was let out a grunt when he was yanked off his feet. He hit the ground hard and was dragged along behind Slocum's thundering horse.

Slocum didn't want to drag the man to death, but he also didn't want him running off to the sheriff. His shoulders began to ache from the strain of pulling Wilkins behind, so he looped the hemp rope around the horn and slowed the headlong pace his sorrel had found so exhilarating. Turning down a side street, Slocum quickly left Forlorn and got into the deserted Utah countryside.

When he was far enough away so that Wilkins's shouts couldn't be heard, Slocum reined back, and the sorrel dug in its heels. The horse's sides heaved from the effort, but Slocum felt the same excitement the horse did. At last he was able to get back at the man for his dirty dealings.

"What are you doing, you stupid son of a bitch? I'll kill you!" Wilkins struggled to get to his feet, but the rope hindered him, and dragging through the streets had ripped both clothing and flesh to bloody ribbons.

"Figured it was apparent what I was doing," Slocum said. "If you need to see more, then we'd better get to it." Slocum jerked hard on the rope and pulled Wilkins off his feet again. Slocum guided his horse under a tree, looking for the right limb. He saw one high up and tossed the loose end over it and quickly grabbed it to refasten it on his saddlehorn.

"I'll fill you so full of holes nobody'll ever recognize you," Wilkins grated out between clenched teeth as he fought to get free of the rope holding his arms to his sides.

Slocum watched for a few seconds, waited until Wilkins untangled the rope from his shoulders and dropped the loop into the dirt, then suddenly put the spurs to his horse. The sorrel neighed and bolted, and the lassoed sharpshooter screamed as his feet were dragged out from under him. Slocum didn't stop the horse's slow, deliberate walk until Wilkins hung upside down a good ten feet off the ground. He swung to and fro slowly like a human pendulum in the wind.

"Have a good night," Slocum said, getting down from his horse and fastening the end around another tree trunk.

"You can't leave me like this. Get me down!" Wilkins fought to reach his feet encircled by the rope but failed and fell back down, only swinging more than he had been. "I'll freeze to death out here."

"No such luck," Slocum said. He rode up and almost looked Wilkins in the eye. The upside down man grabbed for him, but Slocum moved back slightly, and Wilkins missed.

He rode off, Wilkins's curses fading in the wind after only a few hundred yards. Slocum felt as good about helping out as he had since agreeing to join Baron Fenstermacher's Fabulous Continental Circus.

Back in Forlorn, the performance was ending, and people came from the tent smiling and laughing. The show had been a hit. Slocum dismounted, tethered his horse, and stood back eavesdropping on the circus' patrons. They enjoyed the performance more than they had an earlier one over at Sells Brothers Circus.

"We did it, John. It was great. I've never shot better, and Morelli didn't fall from the highwire and and and—" Maddy bubbled over with joy. She ran out of words and just threw her arms around his neck and kissed him hard. He tried to push her back. People might see, and he didn't want to besmirch her reputation through gossip. She took a half step back, her arms still around his neck. Her dark eyes burned with passion.

"Don't worry, John," she said. "Circus people aren't like others."

"People are the same no matter where they are," he said. No class of people was better than any other. The War between the States had been fought over that notion, and Slocum had come to believe it the more he rode through the West.

"You can be so cynical," she said. In a lower voice she said, "I want you to be something else."

Slocum considered what had to be done. Sometime during the night Andre and the other three had to be sneaked back into the jail so the sheriff wouldn't be suspicious come morning. But that could wait. He felt himself responding as Maddy ran her hand through his hair, across his cheek, down his chest, and then even lower. Strong fingers squeezed and urged him to take a few minutes of pleasure.

"Where can we go?" he asked. He knew she didn't have any permanent quarters like many of the others. Maddy simply slept under the stars when they weren't in a town.

"Inside, in the tent."

"But the men working there will—"

"Hush," she said. "They're taking a break and won't be back to strike the tent for an hour or more."

She led him inside. Slocum had reservations, but the lure of the lovely woman was more than he could resist. She was more alive after the great performance than he had ever seen here. Before, she had been morose, living in the past and awash with tormenting memories of her dead husband. But all that was gone now. Slocum thought this must be the real Madeleine Scowcroft peeking out from under long years of mourning, and he liked it.

"Are you sure?" Slocum asked, still worrying about the bustle outside the tent.

"I'm sure," she said, pulling closer to him and kissing him with years of pent-up desire. Slocum returned the kiss, not caring any more who might blunder in and find them in the center ring. He was surprised when Maddy pushed him away, put her fingers into her mouth and let out an earsplitting whistle. Slocum heard her stallion neigh loudly outside the tent.

"What's going on?" he asked. Maddy smiled wickedly and shook her head, silently telling him he'd find out—and that they'd both enjoy the discovery.

The horse came into the tent and trotted over. Slocum saw that it was still saddled from the performance. Then his attention was pulled back to the woman. She kicked off her boots and began skinning out of her tight britches. Slocum sucked in his breath and held it. Seldom had he ever seen a woman this lovely or desirable. She unfastened her vest and let her firm, high breasts bob freely.

"Let me," she said, her fingers touching here and there and making his gunbelt drop to the ground like magic. Maddy didn't stop there. She got his trousers unbuttoned and reached inside, stroking the hardness she found there. "Just right for what I have in mind," she said. "Are you a good horseman, John?"

"Fair to middling good," he allowed, not quite sure what she was getting at.

"Mount up. My horse is strong enough to carry the pair of us." Slocum swung into the saddle, still not certain what Maddy wanted from him. He had to position himself carefully to keep from painfully banging tender parts against the pommel. He didn't have to guess any longer what she had in mind.

Maddy lithely jumped up, facing Slocum. Her strong legs locked around the backs of his and guided his feet into the stirrups for support. Then she lifted up and began wiggling until she found the tip of his quivering manhood.

"You're not going to—" Slocum gasped when Maddy lowered herself around him. He scooted back in the saddle to give her a bit more room in front, but they were locked firmly together. The stallion pawed and snorted and every movement caused tremors to pass through Slocum's body. He couldn't begin to guess what sensations ripped through Maddy as she balanced on horse and man. She closed her eyes and leaned back a bit, a look of ultimate ecstasy on her face.

"Giddyup," she called out, and the stallion began trotting around the ring. She had trained the animal to maintain an even gait during her act. Now she used the powerful beast for something even more exciting. Every time a hoof hit the ground Slocum gulped and tried to hold back. He wouldn't have thought such motion would have robbed him of control this fast.

It did.

He tightened his legs on the horse and reached out to cup both of Maddy's bouncing breasts. The nipples had hardened into coppery buttons that throbbed under his fingers as he pressed down. Her breathing turned ragged, and she gasped out something he didn't understand.

Slocum wasn't going to ask her what she'd said. There was no need because he could see the desire etched in every line of her face. From the bright, rosy flush rising up from her breasts to her shoulders and neck he knew she was locked in the throes of intense desire. Her strong fingers closed on his forearms for support, and she began rising just a bit more than the motion of the horse caused, then slammed down hard to give them both a powerful surge of indescribable pleasure.

"I never knew it could be this good, John. So good, so good!"

Slocum didn't know what the signal was but the horse started circling the ring at a faster pace. The extra speed made the lovemaking all the more intense, Maddy's hips rising and falling even faster. He was pinned to the saddle by her weight, but it didn't matter. If anything, it caused the fires to mount in his loins even faster than usual. Slocum let loose of the twin mounds of succulent flesh bobbing between them and leaned back, thrusting his hips forward and up. The stallion seemed to expect such movement and immediately compensated for it.

Maddy's tanned oval face was a mask of stark delight. She moaned constantly and began moving up and down on Slocum's length even faster, the stallion's motion adding to the woman's. Slocum was content to simply go along for the ride. He forced himself upright again and put his arms around the woman's waist, pulling her close.

Using the stirrups for leverage, he lifted her even farther off the horse's back and drove deeply into her center. All too soon for Slocum's liking, he felt the hot tide rising within him explode outward and spill into Maddy's clinging interior.

He wanted this marvelous feeling to last forever, but all too soon he had turned flaccid, and the woman clung tightly to him, her head against his shoulder. All the while the stallion kept running tirelessly around the ring. Slocum wished he had the animal's incredible strength and endurance.

"Enough," Maddy finally said. Her legs untangled from his and she leaned back. With an agile move, she swung her leg up and over his head and dropped to the ground. Slocum almost fell from the saddle because of the woman's sudden exit. By the time he grabbed the horse's reins and had halted its perpetual circling, Maddy had slithered back into her skintight britches and was putting on her boots.

She looked up at him, her ebony eyes blazing.

"You're flopping around. Better button up," she said.

Slocum pulled the horse to a halt and jumped down to fasten his fly. "That's the most fun I ever had riding bareback."

"Riding bare," she corrected. "I'd left the saddle on."

He wasn't going to argue. He went to Maddy and kissed her again. But Slocum broke off when he remembered he had other matters to attend to first.

"I've got to get Andre and the others back into the jail before morning. I don't want the sheriff finding out we'd switched."

"He doesn't care," Maddy said. "He just counted heads and will be happy as long as it doesn't look as if anyone's escaped." She hugged him even tighter.

Slocum knew that Wilkins wouldn't hang forever in the tree. He might not be able to get himself down, but someone would ride by sooner or later and release the man. Or Wilkins might prove stronger than he looked and be able to pull himself up enough to get his feet free.

"I've got to do it just as soon as Andre gets Trajan settled for the night," Slocum said. "We don't want to get stuck in Forlorn any longer than we have to."

"This was the only performance," Maddy said. "We're due in Orem in three days. This time it ought to be easy getting there. We've got the railroad cars now and don't have to go across country, though we could if we had to."

Slocum didn't bother telling her about his run-in with Wilkins during the performance, but he still worried. He finished strapping on his cross-draw holster to go find Andre and the other three and get them back into the Forlorn jail. He wanted to be out of this jerkwater town at dawn.

"John," she said softly. "Hurry back. I'll be waiting for you."

He nodded, smiling at her. Maybe staying in the town a bit past dawn wouldn't be that bad after all.

9

Slocum awoke, and he couldn't figure out why. He lay flat on his back staring up at the stars occasionally vanishing under a thin layer of clouds, Maddy Scowcroft sound asleep beside him. Slocum sat up and looked around. He had learned to listen to his sixth sense when it warned him something was wrong. Strain as he might, though, he neither heard nor saw anything out of the ordinary. Hours earlier, he had replaced Andre and the others in the town jail without any mishap. The deputy had been so far in his cups that he'd slept through them trooping into the jail, opening the cells, and making the switch. The entire while he had done nothing but snore loudly.

On that score, Slocum knew there wasn't anything more he could do or any reason to worry about the sheriff's wrath. Even if Wilkins got down and rushed into the sheriff, he'd find only the prisoners in the cells he had put in the night before. Whatever gnawed at Slocum's mind lay somewhere else.

He looked down at Maddy. The faint glow of the Milky Way arching across the ink-black sky turned her into something more angelic than human, but Slocum knew this was wrong. What they had done, both in the circus tent mounted on her white stallion and after, was entirely human. Pleasurably so, to his way of thinking.

81

He reached for his Colt and checked it, then rose, scrambled into his trousers and shirt and finally found his boots. He knocked them out from habit, dislodging from the left boot a small scorpion seeking a warm place to spend the night, and then pulled them on. Cold wind whipped down from the high country, but Slocum ignored it. The main tent had been struck and folded, waiting to be loaded on a freight car in the morning. But Slocum saw faint shadows moving nearby, shadows that might be cast by a tall man.

Walking carefully to keep from being heard, he circled and came up on the side nearest the railroad tracks running through the town and past where Baron Fenstermacher had set up the tent.

"Not enough, I tell you," came an angry whisper. "You got to give me another five dollars."

"You're a goddamn robber. You agreed to do a job and now you're backing down." This voice clearly belonged to Clay Wilkins. Slocum peered out from a stack of crates holding various circus paraphernalia waiting for the freight cars to roll up and the roustabouts to load them in the morning.

"I done what I said," the first man whined. "You never said this Slocum fellow would give us any trouble."

Wilkins spat angrily like a stepped-on cat. "I'll take care of him when the time is right."

Slocum kept from laughing out loud. The boy Billy might be able to outshoot Slocum, but Clay Wilkins never could. Even cheating, he wasn't any match, but what worried Slocum more than anything else was what the man had done to the baron's circus before. He was a backstabber and had no conscience about the people he hurt. Slocum had seen his share of men like Wilkins and wasn't going to take much more from him.

"We pulled that stunt with the railroad cars before. I don't know if it'll work again."

"Make it work," Wilkins said in a cold voice, "or you'll regret it."

"I need more money to bribe the engineer."

"You've got the money. The engineer only got half what

you bilked from me. Use that, but get it done. I don't want this circus able to move on. You got that?"

The man mumbled, and Slocum saw the shadows split and go in opposite directions. There wasn't any reason to follow Wilkins. He knew where to find him, but he had to know who was selling out the baron. Slocum drifted like a ghost through the night and came to a small campsite set off some distance from the others. The shadow he had been trailing stopped, knelt, and began working on a small campfire. The flare as it lit momentarily showed the man's face.

Slocum wanted to use his pistol and just put the man out of everyone's misery. Kincaid, the baron's right-hand man, was responsible for the betrayal. He held back to see what the circus' business manager was up to. The man rummaged in his bedroll and finally pulled out a dark wad of what Slocum took to be greenbacks. Kincaid counted a few out and then thrust the roll back into hiding.

He took off, muttering as he went. Slocum stopped for a moment to verify that Kincaid had taken some money. Without counting, Slocum thought there was at least a hundred dollars in the poke. This must be bribe money Kincaid had received from Wilkins to sabotage the circus. He replaced it and went after Kincaid, knowing where the man was most likely headed.

Kincaid made a beeline for the railroad siding where an engine was pulled over, waiting for the baron's freight and animals to be loaded. Slocum circled and got ahead of the man, thinking hard. He wasn't sure what he could do. Baron Fenstermacher valued loyalty and was not likely to believe a man who had been with him for years could sell him out for a few dollars.

The train's crew wasn't too alert, and Slocum didn't see where the engineer slept, but he did see something else that started him thinking. Then he acted without considering his actions. No matter what happened to Kincaid, it was less than the man deserved for his treachery.

Slocum walked over and began working on the locking-bar arrangement on a cage a few yards from the train.

Kincaid heard the clank of metal on metal and paused, wondering who might be out at this time of night.

"What's—" This was all the man got to say before Slocum shoved him hard. Kincaid flailed around, his hand hitting the edge of the cage Slocum had opened. Kincaid shrieked and tried not to lose his balance. Slocum helped him with a second shove, then slammed the door shut behind him.

"What are you doing, Slocum? Let me out. This is a lion!"

"A hungry one, maybe," Slocum said, not enjoying the man's panic but seeing a way to use it. "Too bad you won't get to spend all that money you got off Clay Wilkins."

"What are you talking about, Slocum? This is crazy. Let me out!"

Kincaid rattled the cage door and only caused the sleeping lion to stir. The huge cat stretched, yawned, and then opened one eye to study what had been tossed into its cage.

"Must think you're breakfast," Slocum said. "Don't know what they usually feed the big cats, but raw meat must be a part of their diet. You're finally going to be useful around here."

"Please don't do this. I'm terrified of lions."

"I'll put that on your tombstone, if there's enough left of you to bury. I've heard tell lions chew the bones and break them up into such small pieces there's just not much left."

"What do you want from me?" Kincaid rattled the bars again, but Slocum held the door firmly shut. Slocum saw that the man's cries had roused the camp. He paid no attention because he wanted Kincaid to confess everything.

"A shame you're going to choke that lion on the money you were going to bribe the engineer with."

"Here, take it," Kincaid babbled. He looked back just as the lion roared loudly and shoved itself to its feet. "Let me out. Please, Slocum! I didn't mean to double-cross the baron. Wilkins made me do it. He paid me. Let me out!"

The lion roared again but didn't seem to be paying attention to the new occupant of its cage.

"Baron, I'm sorry," Kincaid shouted. "I didn't want to do it, but I need the money. Wilkins made me do it!"

"What is this?" demanded Baron Fenstermacher, pulling on his gaudy ringmaster's coat as he came to see what the disturbance was. He just stood and stared at his manager inside the cage.

"I bribed the engineer to leave us." Kincaid was beside himself with fear. "Wilkins didn't think we'd make it to Forlorn in time for this performance. Let me out!"

"What were you on your way to do?" Slocum prodded. Kincaid eyed the lion suspiciously, but the animal didn't approach. That didn't keep the trapped man from sweating bullets in his attempt to get out.

"Wilkins wanted me to do it again. He staged the fight that got our men landed in jail. He paid off the sheriff and he paid me to have the engineer pull out right away to strand us here. Let me out!"

Slocum pulled the door open, and Kincaid tumbled out. The frightened man looked up at Slocum with pleading eyes. Slocum took the money Kincaid had clutched in his hand and passed it over to the baron.

"He's got a big wad of money tucked away in his gear, too. Reckon that belongs to the circus since he was working for you when he took it."

"What of him?" someone asked.

"I'd throw him back into the lion's cage," Slocum said, "but the lion's got too much taste to eat him."

"Leo?" A trainer laughed heartily. "This poor old guy's not got a tooth in his head. I got to grind up his meat for him. Even his claws ain't what they used to be."

"Leo? This isn't Simba's cage?" Kincaid sat up and stared at the lion. His face went a pasty white, but Slocum couldn't tell if it was fear or rage.

"Why don't you just start walking?" Slocum suggested. "Baron Fenstermacher might not find out if Simba's got more of an appetite if you make yourself scarce enough. Accidents do happen around a circus."

"I'll get my gear and—"

"Now!" Slocum bellowed. Kincaid jumped and almost

ran, looking back over his shoulder. Slocum spun the cylinder in his Colt Navy to keep the man traveling.

"I never knew he was capable of such a thing," muttered the baron. "Are all my people being bought by the Sells brothers?"

"Put the blame where it ought to lie," Slocum said. "You can't buy an honest man, and there's nothing to say the Sells brothers themselves even know about this. I'd put it all on Clay Wilkins."

"Or Adam Bogardus," Maddy said hotly. "Wilkins is only his damnable pawn. The captain wants to ruin us and always has because he knows I can outshoot any of his team—and I sure as hell can outshoot him, given half a chance!"

"Find the engineer and get your gear loaded," Slocum suggested. He didn't want Wilkins to find out about Kincaid's failure and try something more to stop them.

"What of Andre and the others? They still reside in the town's jail," said the baron.

"I'll see to it. You get moving," Slocum said. The sun poked up over distant mountains, heralding a new day. Maddy started to accompany him but he waved her back. She was hot-headed and might throw fuel onto a fire Slocum wanted to bank.

It took more than an hour for Slocum to spring the circus workers from the jail. Andre came out, stretched, and smiled at Slocum. The other performers who had put on such a fine show the night before also grinned broadly. They had put one over on the sheriff, and this united them more than ever—and it was Slocum's credentials for membership in their exclusive club.

Slocum and the others returned to the railroad in time to finish loading the last of the equipment. Andre herded Trajan onto a flatcar and made sure his huge gray ward was properly situated, then the railroad took off for their next performance.

It took three days for them to arrive in Orem, Utah, and Slocum's heart sank when he saw that the Sells Brothers Circus had somehow beaten them into town. Slocum remembered how they had spent six hours in a siding the night before; this might have given the rival circus the chance to slip by them because Baron Fenstermacher's Fabulous Continental Circus had left Forlorn hours ahead.

"Rat bills," grumbled the baron. "They have given out hundreds of them. We must counter them. We will give out half-price passes." He continued mumbling to himself as he walked off.

"He's still shaken by Kincaid," Maddy told Slocum. "Kincaid used to take care of many of the details the baron has to now, and it's wearing him down."

"There's no need for flyers if you think on it," Slocum said. "Remember the crowd when we challenged the Bogardus Shooting Team to a match? Let's do it again."

"We don't have the money to make it worthwhile," Maddy said.

"There's the money we got off Kincaid. Why not use Wilkins's money against him?"

"The baron hasn't touched a nickel of it," Maddy said, considering what he said. "He told me Kincaid had over a hundred dollars in greenbacks. Blood money," she almost snarled. "It makes me furious thinking he was profiting by selling us out to Wilkins." Maddy shook all over like a wet dog, then wrapped her arms tightly around herself as if suddenly cold.

"Twenty-dollar bets make for plenty of interest." Slocum wanted another crack at the fourteen-year-old Billy. The boy was damned good but Slocum knew what to expect now in a match. He was a good shot, but this kind of marksmanship was new to him.

"Let's do it," Maddy said with a sudden flash of excitement. She fetched her rifle and dropped a box of shells into her pocket, matching the bulge in her other pocket. Slocum got his Winchester from its sheath and checked the sights. He was ready to take on the world, and that included Billy.

The Sells Brothers Circus was set up across town. Slocum and Maddy got there about the time the shooting team was beginning to knock over clay pipes and blow apart the feather-filled glass targets. Slocum and Maddy spent a few minutes working through the crowd, planting the seeds of a real contest so they would be right on the spot when the people of Orem demanded more.

"A shoot-out," Slocum called. "Let's go head-to-head. Ten dollars says I can beat the boy."

"Ten? Is that all you have?" demanded Wilkins, working the crowd. "We'd hate to take your money if it'd leave you destitute."

"Fifteen," Maddy chimed in.

"Twenty," Slocum said, upping her bid before Wilkins had a chance to reply. "Or doesn't Captain Bogardus think his men can win such a big bet?"

"You wanted to shoot against Billy," Wilkins said, "but the boy's under the weather with just a touch of the ague. Otherwise I'd let him finish you off."

"How about you, Wilkins? I'll take *you* on, if you aren't scared that a woman'll beat you." Maddy pushed to the front of the crowd and loudly said, "I'm the sharpshooter with Baron Fenstermacher's circus, a real show. We're not some namby-pamby—"

"Get the targets," snapped Wilkins. "We'll shoot it out for fifty dollars."

Slocum silently handed over the portion of Kincaid's money to Maddy, who added it to the money she already had. A local resident was chosen to hold the wager, which brought even more people over to watch. But Slocum started to worry when he loudly suggested that a few of the towns-people inspect the glass targets and Wilkins didn't object.

"There's something wrong," he told Maddy. "Wilkins agreed too quickly to checking the glass balls. He's got some other scheme cooking."

"He's just over-confident about his ability," she said, putting her spare shells on a low table. "I'll beat him before we get to one hundred rounds."

Slocum wasn't so sure. The smirk on Wilkins's face told him the contest was somehow rigged, but he couldn't figure out how. He checked dozens of the targets and saw to it that

Maddy got hers from the same box Wilkins used.

"You two ready to do some shootin'?" asked the man holding the bet. "Then get on down and do it!"

The contest began slowly, the targets being tossed into the air at measured intervals, but both Wilkins and Maddy found this too confining. When each had broken twenty of the glass balls and sent more than a hen's worth of feathers floating down over the crowd, they indicated they wanted a quicker pace.

The crowd grew when the two reached fifty targets each, and Slocum was sure most of the town had come by the time Maddy reached one hundred. The men were astounded at her sharpshooting skills as well as her beauty. The women weren't as impressed with the shooting, and Slocum saw more than one eyeing Maddy with envy and a touch of jealously because of the way their men watched her so intently.

Slocum watched Wilkins closely and saw that the man was straining after a hundred and twenty-five targets. Maddy looked as if she was just settling down. Slocum worked through the crowd and found it impossible to get odds against Maddy. Public sentiment was on her side. And Slocum kept worrying. Clay Wilkins was struggling with every shot but not looking panicked about it.

The day's heat began to take its toll after two hundred targets. Maddy was visibly tiring, but Wilkins was in no better condition. By two hundred and fifty Maddy was shaking from strain. And then it happened. She missed.

"If I break this one, the match is over," Wilkins said.

"And if you miss it, the contest goes on," Slocum called out to get the man's goat. He checked the target Wilkins was going to use, just to be sure he hadn't sneaked in a broken one.

Wilkins took his time, wiping his face with a bandanna. He emptied his rifle and carefully loaded in a single shell before saying, "This is all I'll need to win."

The target arced into the air, gleaming brightly. Wilkins swung, shot and broke the sphere, bringing down a rain of feathers. A hush settled over the crowd, then someone cheered.

"The Bogardus Shooting Team!" Wilkins cried, prancing like some dandy in his colorful uniform. "Come see us perform acts of astounding marksmanship inside the big tent at the Sells Brothers Circus!" He dropped his rifle on the table and came over, holding out his hand to the man holding the wager. The money quickly vanished into Wilkins's pocket. He smiled wickedly and said to Slocum, "You'll never beat me. You're not good enough, you're not smart enough." He spun and went to work the crowd some more.

Slocum didn't know how it had happened but Wilkins had rigged the contest again. Everything about the way the man acted screamed it to him. But how?

10

The evening performance was a disaster. The Sells Brothers Circus had arrived ahead of the baron and had already milked most of the money from the townspeople. Even worse, after Wilkins beat Maddy in the disastrous afternoon shoot-out, the few that might have attended Baron Fenstermacher's circus stayed away.

"We need to keep people coming in," Maddy said glumly. "The baron's talking about changing over to a sideshow."

"You mean with freaks and the like?" Slocum scratched his head. There weren't bearded women or midgets with the circus because the baron thought real entertainment lay in skills both human and animal.

"We'd have to use makeup. I played a wild woman from Borneo once, a couple years ago when times were really hard." Maddy shivered. "We were broke and didn't have money to get on to our next engagement. If winter had caught us, we'd've been stranded, and the circus would have disbanded. I had to pretend to eat raw meat."

"There must be another way of getting the crowds in. Maybe when the other circus moves on the people will flock in." Even as he spoke, Slocum knew what was wrong with this idea.

Maddy shook her head and said, "It doesn't work that way. There's never surplus money in a small town. The circus that gets to town first will always take most of the spare change. We might get a few dimes but it won't be enough to cover expenses."

"And the Sells Brothers Circus train is ahead of ours on the tracks," said Slocum. "That means they'll leave first and get to the next town down the line and wring every penny out of it before we get there." The situation looked bleaker by the minute.

"It's no coincidence they have the same schedule we do," Maddy said bitterly. "It has to be Kincaid's doing. We'll be living down his treachery for quite a while—maybe until the circus goes bankrupt."

"Kincaid's gone and we're still here," Slocum said. "Maybe staying an extra day or two will work out. If the baron telegraphs ahead and changes the schedule, we can go to some other town along the railroad."

Maddy laughed and it wasn't pleasant. "This is Utah. There aren't any spurs worth mentioning off the main line. Forlorn was well named."

"This is Orem," Slocum said, distracted. Two of the crew from the baron's railroad engine were talking to him. The baron bobbed up and down like a cork in a turbulent stream, getting angrier by the second. Slocum motioned for Maddy to stay put and went to eavesdrop.

"There's nothing we can do. We got a telegraph off to bring us in a new piston, but till it gets here, we ain't budging."

"This is impossible," the baron raged. "We must go tomorrow."

"Tomorrow ain't gonna do it, Baron," the engineer said. "We're lookin' at a minimum of three days to get the part in from the depot and maybe longer. That piston done split wide open. No matter how much we stoke the old boiler, there's nothin' to make the wheels turn. We're stuck here."

"Get a blacksmith. Have it fixed. We cannot stay here for this long a time!"

"Orem's a nice little village, Baron. Won't be so bad coolin' your heels while we're waitin'." The engineer scratched himself and looked over his shoulder in the direction of a small café. It didn't take Slocum much guessing to know where the local saloon was. Railroad men would know such things.

"We cannot stay," the baron protested. Slocum went up and put his hand on the agitated nobleman's shoulder.

"Calm down, Baron. We can use the wait to work on new acts."

"New acts? What are you saying, Slocum?"

Slocum guided the man away from the engineer and his assistant oiler to a spot where they wouldn't be overheard.

"Getting to the next town ahead of the Sells brothers might keep the circus going, wouldn't it?" Slocum saw the answer on the baron's face. It meant the difference between survival and bankruptcy.

"Get everything packed and ready to load just after sunset," Slocum said.

"But there is another show to put on."

"Forget it. Maddy said there's not likely to be many customers since the Sells Brothers Circus is having a second night and is giving discounted tickets to those who showed up yesterday."

"The show must go on," the baron said resolutely.

"Then get everything ready for transport at sundown while Wilkins and the others are putting on their show."

The baron looked curiously at Slocum and said, "There is this matter of the piston. We must wait for it."

"It won't get here until it gets here," Slocum allowed. "Maybe we can help matters by wishing real hard and doing some planning on our own. You go on with the sideshow you were planning. Get flyers out, do your usual advertising."

"But we are to have the tent and animals ready for transport at sundown," the baron said. He went off in a daze, shaking his head and wondering what Slocum was doing. But Slocum was pleased that the circus owner didn't question him too closely. He might not like what was going to happen.

Slocum returned to the siding for a quick look at the two trains. He counted cars and saw that the Sells Brothers Circus engine pulled fourteen freight cars in addition to two passenger cars. The animals rode in style, especially their elephant, which had a special car all to itself. Slocum knew the hardship that Trajan had endured on this trip and thought how fitting it was for the beast to make the next leg of the trip in such relative comfort.

Slocum walked along the crowded tracks and saw the train immediately behind it, trapped until the other engine and cars pulled out. Business along this deserted railroad route couldn't be too great or the trains sitting on the main line would block routine traffic. He doubted that amounted to a hill of beans or there would be a siding where the trains could pull off.

He looked over the broken piston on the baron's train and saw that the engineer hadn't been lying about its condition. More important to Slocum, the damage had obviously happened owing to the piston simply breaking and not from any sabotage on Wilkins's part. Slocum didn't trust the engineer one whit since he had been so easily bought by Kincaid, but this time the man didn't have to get money to hold up progress on the baron's circus.

Slocum went off, whistling tunelessly as plans turned over and over in his head. He saw Wilkins standing across the dusty road, but the sharpshooter wasn't watching the trains. The hatchet-faced man was intent on the baron's preparations for the sideshow attractions. The crooked grin on Wilkins's face told Slocum everything he needed to know. Wilkins was buying the obvious helplessness of the baron's position, the Sells Brothers Circus having upstaged him at every turn.

But how had Wilkins beaten Maddy in the shoot-out? That kept eating away at Slocum. There had been some trickery, and he had missed it. He had even toyed with the idea that Billy was hidden somewhere doing the shooting for Wilkins, but this didn't wash. Entire cartridges had gone into Wilkins's Winchester, and only spent brass came out when he levered in the next round. Even that final shot had been honest—or had appeared honest.

Slocum had checked the spent brass and had found nothing amiss. The sharp smell of gunpowder showed a bullet had been fired, and he had looked carefully to be sure the round wasn't just a blank.

Wilkins had outshot Maddy. How?

Slocum shook off worrying on it any more. He had better things to do. He slipped into the general store and watched Wilkins until the sharpshooter had satisfied himself that the baron wasn't going to mount any competition for the evening show.

"Help you, sonny?" The proprietor of the store looked up from a game of dominoes in the back. The men he played with didn't even bother turning. They were too intent on their game of forty-two to much care.

"Just looking, thank you," Slocum said. He hurried out of the store and followed Wilkins back to the circus. The man spoke a few minutes with young Billy and the other sharpshooter on the Bogardus team—Slocum remembered Wilkins calling him Dellman. Clay Wilkins then vanished into the huge tent flapping in the cold, hard breeze from the mountains. Slocum considered going in to spy further on Wilkins and decided against it. The people were already lining up to buy their tickets for the evening show. Damned few would be seeing the pathetic sensationalistic sideshow Baron Fenstermacher would offer. This interest in the Sells Brothers Circus suited Slocum just fine. It gave him a chance to get one up on Wilkins again.

The baron had set up a few smaller tents and erected garish signs in front of them. Slocum poked his head into the first one and saw two of the roustabouts working to put a fake dog's head onto an obviously disgruntled animal trainer.

"Jojo the Dogfaced Boy," the trainer called out. "I can bark like a dog and yet I can cipher and answer questions, only a nickel, come on in, only a nickel!" He laughed without humor and turned to let the men continue putting the heavy makeup on him. Slocum wondered how anyone could go from handling jungle cats to this charade. It was completely degrading.

"Like me? Want to see me eat some raw meat?"

Slocum turned and saw dark eyes boring into him. In spite of the makeup and the animal furs, he knew this was Maddy.

"I've had better dinners," he said, "but maybe for you I'll make an exception. Just don't go eating Jojo in there." Slocum jerked his thumb back in the direction of the tent.

Maddy laughed. "Joshua and I get along just fine, but we're not on that good of terms."

"Don't be," Slocum warned with mock severity. He looked up and saw the sun dipping low in the west. When they got moving, they'd have to do everything fast. "You ready to leave this town?"

"But the piston's broke on the locomotive," Maddy said. "We're stuck here for days."

"Pass the word that we're pulling out in a couple hours. Keep your gear packed and ready to load."

"What's going on, John?"

"Later," he said, bending over and giving Maddy a quick kiss. He made a face and added, "That's the first time I ever kissed a wild girl from Borneo."

"Let's hope it's your last."

"Get ready to move out soon." He touched her cheek fleetingly and came away with heavy smears of brown paint. Then he was off to see about the rest of his scheme. The baron would be a willing accomplice but the task at hand rested squarely on Slocum's shoulders.

Slocum gathered the roustabouts as he went through the encampment and pointed to the cages of animals and heavy crates holding their equipment. The big tent had been bundled up and stood in a heap taller than Slocum and needed a dozen strong men to move it. He motioned for them to begin loading onto the lead train—the Sells Brothers Circus train.

"What's going on there?" came an aggrieved voice. "You can't load up. We're not ready for it, not till tomorrow morning."

"This town's a dud," Slocum said, "so the boss decided to get us on the next stop tonight. If you were going to be ready to move out in the morning, why aren't you ready to go now?"

"Didn't say we weren't ready, just said we didn't expect you till dawn or thereabouts." The engineer peered nearsightedly at the workmen heaving the crates into the freight cars. "Don't look like the equipment we brought in."

"Can you keep a secret?" Slocum asked, putting his arm around the engineer's shoulders and steering him away. "We bought out the rival circus."

The engineer peered up at him and took off his cap, running his fingers through his greasy hair. "The devil you say. You don't look familiar. Who be ye?"

"Used to work for the baron's circus," Slocum said, "but the Sells brothers made me a better offer. I'm sort of head wrangler for the outfit now."

"What became of Kincaid? I remember him with that shooting fellow."

"Wilkins?" Slocum struggled to keep from spitting out the name as if it had turned to acid on his tongue. "Wilkins and I are working together like this." Slocum held up crossed fingers. "But you know how it's set up. I work for the circus, not Captain Bogardus."

"If you want to roll out early, I reckon we can do our best. My crew . . ." The engineer left the sentence dangling, and Slocum knew what the problem was. He had spent some of the day at the small café that doubled as a saloon.

"Let me check with my men. Be right back," Slocum said. He found the small box he had fixed up earlier for this situation and hefted it. Gurgling and sloshing all the way, Slocum lugged it back to the engineer. "This might make work go a little smoother," he said.

The engineer looked in and grinned, showing broken front teeth. "They'll be flyin' to get this kind of hooch," he said. "You want to roll in an hour, we'll be gone in an hour and to Wisdom by noon."

Slocum oversaw the loading, then signaled that it was time to strike the tents with the sideshow. Maddy and the others didn't even bother taking off their makeup. They just climbed aboard with Baron Fenstermacher, who gave the all-clear signal to Slocum.

"Steam on out of here," he told the engineer, who had imbibed heavily of Slocum's hooch. The man hooted and howled as he climbed into the engine cab. He shouted something Slocum didn't understand, and his boiler stokers began working frantically, shoveling in first a few sticks of wood and then shovelfuls of coal. In less than fifteen minutes the boilers were hot and up to steam, and the train was pulling out of Orem on its way to Wisdom.

And Wilkins and the rest of the Sells Brothers Circus was stranded for at least three days. That alone made this small victory sweet for Slocum.

11

"No competition," gloated Baron Fenstermacher. "The whole town is ours for the plucking." He dropped to the ground as the train screeched to a halt and threw his arms high in the air in a gesture of triumph. "This is as it ought to be. No damnable Sells Brothers to steal our glory."

Maddy came up close behind Slocum and put her hand on his shoulder. "This is the happiest I've seen him in months. The town is perfect for us—bored and thriving, and the locals are friendly."

She seemed to be right. The townspeople stood along the railroad tracks, cheering and carrying on. Trajan trumpeted and brought an even bigger response from the crowd. Andre climbed onto Trajan's back and was the first off the train after the baron had jumped down. The elephant instantly became the center of attention, and the baron only smiled more broadly. One by one the circus crew got off the train, stretched, and started looking around for a good place to set up.

"Kincaid usually haggled with the mayor over permits, leases, and the like," Maddy said. "Sometimes he paid the bribes needed to get permission for the show. I reckon I'd better see to finding a patch of land for us to rent for a day or two. Molly Bailey down in Texas buys land wherever she takes her circus so they'll always have a place."

"Must run her a fair amount," Slocum observed, thinking the Bailey circus was a damned sight more profitable than the baron's.

"Most towns don't take too kindly to people just passing through, and circus people have a reputation for being loose." Her dark eyes danced when she said this. "Molly let the churches hold their socials and other local get-togethers on the property when the circus wasn't in town. And she was always right generous about paying for everything that was busted up by her roustabouts."

Baron Fenstermacher's Fabulous Continental Circus was obviously far different because Slocum hadn't seen any sign that the roustabouts or performers got the least bit wild when they weren't working. For the most part they'd always been on the move, never staying in one place long enough to get into real trouble. He didn't consider the hick-town sheriff arresting Andre and the others to be serious because that had been Wilkins's doing.

"I'll go with you to get the use of some land for the tent," he said. Slocum trailed along, wondering if the mayor would have any trouble dealing with a woman. The circus world was different from general society. Male or female didn't matter much to the baron's troupe. They treated everybody according to the respect they'd earned, but Slocum had seen bankers and other men get all condescending when a woman tried to conduct business.

He wasn't too surprised when Maddy proved more than a match for the mayor and two of his aldermen when it came down to dickering, and she got the free use of land in exchange for twenty free tickets. The politicians would pass them out to family, friends, and those they wanted to influence, and it wouldn't cost them anything. And the baron got a chance to earn real money.

The parade went well, with most of the town gathering to watch what the circus promised to show that evening. Leo the toothless lion roared and frightened the more impressionable along the town's main street, Morelli ate fire and drew some attention, Maddy looked utterly fetching on her white stallion, but Trajan was the most popular part of the parade. Without exception, the people fell into awed silence at the size of the elephant, then whispered excitedly when it passed by.

Slocum didn't spend much time at the parade. He found himself falling into Kincaid's old job, overseeing the business details that Baron Fenstermacher couldn't attend to while he was getting the animals settled. The last of the equipment was pulled off the freight cars when he saw the florid, bulbous-nosed engineer storming along, waving a sheet of yellow paper in his hand.

"What's the meaning of this?" the engineer roared. "You aren't the right people. You aren't the Sells Brothers Circus like you said." He waved the telegram around some more, then shoved it into Slocum's face. Slocum made sure the last of the crates and all the animals had been unloaded from the train before turning his attention to the angry railroad engineer. He took the telegram and read it quickly. It was about what he'd expected.

"There does seem to be a mistake. I reckon we took the wrong train."

"The other train's got a busted piston. They can't get out of Orem for another day, and they was supposed to be the ones putting on the show here in Wisdom. What you got to say about that?"

"You could go back for them," Slocum suggested. "Or you could just stay on and wait for them to catch up. Since we got on the wrong train, I don't see any reason for them not to use ours."

"They're raisin' holy hell," the engineer shouted. "They want my head for this. You lied to me."

"Nothing I said was a lie," Slocum replied. "Kincaid isn't with the baron any longer, and I'm taking over his work."

"You said the two circuses were working together. You claimed the Sells bought out the baron."

"Traveling together. That's what I said. You might have misunderstood. I seem to remember there was a powerful lot of noise along those tracks back in Orem. The other locomotive was venting steam, maybe, or there was heavy pounding somewhere nearby." Slocum knew exactly what he'd told the engineer. All he wanted was to keep the railroad officials from getting the law down on the baron for the deception. The circus needed the Wisdom show to pay its bills.

"There'll be hell to pay, mark my words," grumbled the engineer.

"Seems a shame for this to happen. Why don't you and your men have a drink or two on the baron?" Slocum peeled off the last of the illicit greenbacks taken from Kincaid and passed them to the engineer. He didn't much care if the man kept the money or used it to get his crew drunk. Stalling was the best Slocum could do for the circus.

"Well," the engineer said, "don't guess there's anything wrong with that." He took the money and stashed it in a high pocket on his overalls. Licking his lips, he turned and walked off. Slocum was tempted to follow and see what the engineer did with the money, but he held back. He had work to do getting everything set up. At least he had gotten the circus to Wisdom ahead of the Sells brothers. That ought to be good enough for any single day's work.

"A great gate, Mr. Slocum, a great performance, everyone's happy. *I'm* happy." Baron Fenstermacher was more cheerful than Slocum had ever seen him. Success was always sweet.

"The second performance ought to do well, also," Maddy said, smiling from ear to ear. Slocum had seen part of her act and wondered if it was possible for any human to shoot better than she had. The stallion had been a part of it, keeping a steady gait, but Maddy's marksmanship had been unrivaled. Slocum was a good shot, but he wasn't the showman Maddy was, especially from horseback. And he could never use six-shooters in each hand with the accuracy she had.

"They're coming to see you," Slocum said, letting his own opinions show.

Maddy shook her head and caused a small cloud of midnight dark hair to swirl around her tanned face. "The animals. They're coming for them. Andre's never worked better with Trajan."

The baron and Maddy discussed what had gone best and what needed change. Slocum saw that a few extra dollars could benefit the circus greatly, buying new uniforms, possibly hiring professional musicians instead of relying on the performers not on stage to blow the trumpets and bang on the drums, and even a better collection of exotic animals was mentioned. Slocum knew that success bred success. He was grateful to have helped out, but where was his future?

Staying with the circus wasn't for him. He didn't mind doing some of the job Kincaid had performed for the baron, but the thought of keeping on with it for months or even years, made him itch. He belonged under the stars, riding alone, doing whatever he pleased when he pleased. Whether that solitary future included someone like Maddy, he couldn't say. She lived for her performances and came completely alive while shooting. He couldn't offer her the center ring and hundreds of cheering fans.

"What was that?" Maddy demanded. She turned and looked outside the tent into the dark. Slocum saw nothing but heard the disturbance that had alerted the woman.

"Stay here," he said. "I'll find out what's going on." Slocum heard the baron say something more to Maddy, then followed closely. Slocum paused for a moment to let his eyes adjust to the night. The baron barreled past and into the middle of a fight.

"There you are, you little son of a bitch. How dare you steal our train like that?"

Slocum yelled for the baron to duck but he was too late. Clay Wilkins swung and connected solidly with Baron Fenstermacher's chin. The baron's head snapped up and he stumbled, falling into the tent flat on his back.

"We lost money on this gig because of you, you little—" Wilkins shut up suddenly when Slocum stepped over the baron and faced the sharpshooter. Wilkins's rage didn't diminish when he saw Slocum.

"You. I might have known you were still with him."
Wilkins let out a bull roar and attacked.

Slocum ducked under a poorly aimed punch, stepped forward, and drove his fist as hard as he could into Wilkins's belly. The man folded like a bad poker hand and dropped to his knees. Slocum never hesitated. He took a half-step back, wound up, and kicked, the tip of his boot connecting squarely with Wilkins's chin. The sharpshooter tumbled to the side, unconscious. Then all hell broke loose around Slocum. He was shoved and pushed, and men tried to pummel him. He rode the storm of fighting men like a leaf floating on a turbulent river.

The report from a Winchester froze everyone. Maddy swung the rifle around, cocking it again. This time she lowered it and aimed into the crowd.

"Which of you is first to get a bullet in his gut?"

The men from the Sells Brothers Circus backed off, hands going into the air. They knew Maddy's prowess with a rifle and didn't want to cross her.

"Take that worm with you," she said, pointing the rifle at Wilkins's prone form. Two men pulled the groggy Wilkins to his feet. Dazed and muttering incoherently, the sharpshooter staggered off.

"That's about all I've come to expect from him," Maddy said. "Always using his fists instead of his brains." She fired into the air to lend a little more speed to the departure. Satisfied, she bent and helped the baron sit up.

Slocum watched Wilkins and the others leave, wondering why they'd come over to start a fight. Unlike Maddy, he gave Wilkins credit for more sense than to do something pointless. He remembered all too well what had happened after their last fight, but the law seemed absent and not inclined to jail anyone disturbing the peace.

He shrugged it off. Maddy might be right.

The final performance drew even more of a crowd than the earlier one. Slocum was pleased to see that the tables had been turned on the Sells Brothers Circus and Clay Wilkins. The baron had arrived in Wisdom first and had gotten the attention needed to bring people into his show. A second circus performing was too costly, even if the animals were more varied and more energetic than the long-in-the-tooth beasts the baron exhibited. Somehow Wilkins and a few of the others had made it to Wisdom, leaving the rest of their circus behind. Slocum didn't think it would be long before they arrived—but it would be too late.

The crowd was filing out, chattering gaily, and telling each other how they had enjoyed the show. Slocum basked in this reflected glory. He had worked as Maddy's assistant setting up her targets and had even let her shoot a clay pipe from his teeth, but he still wasn't comfortable being the center of attention of so many people. Old habits died hard.

"How did it go, John?" Maddy asked, bubbling with glee.

"You know how it went. They loved every second of it, even Leo and his toothless roaring."

"I wish the performances were all this good. We used to have more like this than not, until the Sells Brothers Circus started competing head-to-head with us."

"You can beat them at their own game. The way Wilkins caved in shows that."

"I want him, John. I want him bad—but even more, I want a match with Captain Bogardus."

"Where is Bogardus? I keep hearing about him, but he doesn't travel with his own shooting team."

Maddy frowned and thought for a few seconds before saying, "I've heard rumors that he's on his way to rejoin the circus. He's been back East to drum up support."

"Financial support?"

"Probably. Even when we do well, there are lean times. Not every town greets us like Wisdom. For that matter, all the Utah towns have been real good to us. Most look at us as some kind of criminals bent on robbing them blind."

Gunshots sounded down the street. Slocum didn't think too much of it. Cowboys with too much liquor in their bellies let off steam by shooting at the sky. Sometimes they shot at one another but seldom hit anything. Slocum had heard of saloon gunfights where two drunks had emptied their six-shooters and hadn't hit anything but mirrors, plate-glass windows, and a few bottles sitting behind the bar.

The loud and persistent shouts from the direction of the town jail caused Slocum to pay more attention. The sheriff and a deputy boiled out, shotguns preceding them. A few seconds later the shotguns roared and more people began contributing to the confusion.

"Must be important," Maddy said. "I'd checked earlier. Those are the only two lawmen Wisdom has, except for a part-time deputy named Lucas."

Slocum wasn't particularly interested until the sheriff and his deputy came storming up. He turned to them and looked down the bores of two double-barreled shotguns.

"What's wrong, Sheriff?"

"You're under arrest, Slocum. For bank robbery!"

12

"What are you talking about?" Maddy demanded. "Slocum's been here throughout the performance."

"We got an eyewitness," the sheriff said. Slocum studied the man and saw he wasn't the kind prone to argument. The set of the sheriff's jaw, the way his finger was white with strain on the twin triggers of the shotgun, and the way he had his feet planted securely told how much he meant business. He was a tad on the fleshy side, but underneath the flab rode more than his fair share of muscle, Slocum saw. This wasn't the kind of man to cross. "And there's more."

"I was here in the tent, just as Miss Scowcroft said. Any of a couple dozen men will vouch for me, too."

"We know how you circus folks are. You stick together. But we got you dead to rights."

Slocum considered trying to make a break for it. Being railroaded for a robbery he didn't commit was sure to bring an investigation into his past. A Wanted poster or two would turn up, and that meant he'd be headed for the gallows. The sheriff might be distracted, if only for an instant. Slocum was quick enough on the draw to take care of him, but not both lawmen.

The alert deputy had moved to the side, making it impossible for Slocum to gun both him and the sheriff, no matter how fast on the draw he was. And if this wasn't enough to keep him from trying, more than a dozen townspeople had gathered to form a circle around them. One or two of them had six-shooters slung at their sides and were nervously fingering the butts, waiting to see if their lawman needed help.

Busting free would mean Slocum had to cut down one or two of them. He'd do it if the choice was swinging from a juniper limb, but it might not come to that. He had said Wilkins's big failing was not using his head. This had to be a case of mistaken identity.

"I was here, Sheriff," Slocum said. "Your witness just got me confused with whoever did rob the bank."

"I doubt it," the sheriff said, scowling hard as if this would make him confess everything. "What time is it, Slocum?"

"Time?" Slocum reached for his vest pocket where he carried Robert's watch. It was his only legacy of a brother killed during the war's most ill-conceived battle. The pocket was empty, but not as empty as Slocum felt inside.

The sheriff held up the watch and let it spin slowly so the gold back caught the light from inside the tent. "It says Robert Slocum on the back. Your father? Maybe a brother?"

"Brother," Slocum said, mind racing. He had the watch during the first show. He remembered looking at it just before helping Maddy with her act. The only time he could have lost it was during the fracas Wilkins had started by knocking out the baron.

"I lost it during a fight earlier tonight."

"A pickpocket!" cried Maddy. "Someone picked your pocket!"

"That's pretty farfetched," the sheriff said. "I found the watch inside the bank, right there on the floor as plain as the nose on your face. And you were seen leaving with the money."

"Who's the witness?" Slocum wasn't in the least surprised to see Clay Wilkins step forward.

"He's the one, Sheriff. I knew there was something crooked about him. He's as bad as the rest of them."

"He's lying," Maddy said hotly, as if it would matter. "He wants to ruin us, and John's been helping out."

"Don't much care about what's going on between you and him," the sheriff said, "but I do care about the bank gettin' robbed. What about it, Lucas?" The sheriff looked toward a man carrying a small bag who had pushed his way through the ever larger crowd.

"Got it, Sheriff Mallory. It looks to be all the money what was taken. As soon as Mr. Prescott makes a count, we'll know, but this is a powerful lot for his kind to be carrying."

"It was planted!" Maddy protested.

"Lady, you're makin' me think you're involved in this muddle. If you don't want to be tossed into the cell beside his, you button that lip of yours."

"It'll be all right, Maddy," Slocum said, still looking for a way out of his predicament. He didn't see one. With the woman and others in the circus so close, he didn't dare try shooting his way clear. Too many innocent people would get cut down by the sheriff's and deputy's shotgun blasts.

"That's smart, Slocum," the sheriff said. "You don't look like the rest of them circus people."

"What's that mean?"

"The way the butt of your six-shooter is worn, I'd say you're mighty quick on the draw. Maybe that's how you make your living—by robbing and shooting others."

"If it is, I don't do it by shooting anyone in the back." Slocum glared at Wilkins, who said nothing. But the smirk on his face told the whole sordid story to anybody who saw it. The sheriff just didn't happen to look in Wilkins's direction; he was too occupied with keeping Slocum covered with the shotgun. Slocum surrendered his Colt Navy and went toward the jail, still trying to figure how he was going to get free. There didn't seem to be any way out.

Sheriff Mallory put Slocum into a secure cell. However he was going to get out of here, it wasn't going to be by tunneling or prying loose a bar. This was the tightest prison Slocum had seen in some time.

He heard the sheriff and the deputy talking in the outer office, then heard someone else enter. An argument went on for a few minutes, then quieted down. Slocum wished for a cell with a window so he could look out back of the jail, but Mallory had put him in an end cell with no exit other than the securely locked door. With nothing else to do, Slocum lay back on the hard cot and stared at the ceiling.

An hour later he heard another commotion in the office. He sat up, wondering what was going on. Sheriff Mallory shouted, and the deputy barked orders, and Slocum got the feeling that neither of them was having any luck doing whatever needed doing. When he heard Maddy's voice from out in the street, he knew she was trying again to get him free.

Slocum stood and went to the bars, his hands gripping them. Whatever she was trying, it was a damnfool thing to do and would only make matters worse. He started to call out when Trajan trumpeted and a man shrieked in fear. Slocum rattled the bars and shouted. He had no idea what was going on outside but a gut feeling told him he was the only one who could control it.

The door to the outer office flew open, and the sheriff stomped in. He opened the door and then drew his six-shooter. "Don't try anything funny, Slocum. I want you to try to make some sense of what's going on outside."

"I'm just your prisoner," Slocum said. "Trying to explain things hasn't done me any good before."

"You know those people. God, I hope you do." Mallory motioned Slocum to the office. Maddy stood there, hands on hips, a determined look on her face. The sheriff said something about women wearing britches, but Maddy didn't hear. She was too resolute. The elephant trumpeted again, and a man's weak cry for mercy hung in the air.

"We got him, I tell you, Sheriff. You've got to listen to an honest confession."

"Who's doing the confessing?" Slocum asked. No matter what Maddy did to him, Slocum couldn't see Clay Wilkins confessing to everything he had done to the baron's circus.

"Dellman," she said. "Wilkins's no-good assistant. He was the one who put the money in your gear, John. And he was the one who pickpocketed your watch during the fight."

"That's all hearsay," the sheriff said. "Your word ain't any better than Wilkins's, and we got evidence."

"Outside," Maddy said. "Listen to Dellman's confession with your own ears."

The sheriff motioned Slocum to go on out. The deputy watched intently, his shotgun never swinging away from Slocum's belly. If Slocum wanted to make a break for it, he had to get the shotgun off him. But when he stepped outside the jail, he had to laugh. Andre rode on Trajan's back, and the elephant's trunk was wrapped securely around a kicking, fighting Dellman.

Wilkins's assistant tried vainly to escape, but the elephant had him trapped too tightly. Maddy went to Dellman and whacked him with the flat of her hand.

"Tell the sheriff what you already told us. Tell him everything."

Dellman was like a cracked dam suddenly giving way and releasing a torrent of water. He was barely coherent as he blurted everything that Clay Wilkins had done to stop Baron Fenstermacher and how they had worked together to frame Slocum. Whenever he slowed, Andre tapped Trajan's head, and the elephant lifted the feckless sharpshooter even higher off the ground and shook just a little harder. This never failed to release a new torrent of acknowledging guilt.

"Put him down," Maddy ordered when Dellman had finished with his rushed confession. Trajan dumped the man in the nearest watering trough, then sucked noisily to drink his fill. Forcing a human to tell the truth was thirsty work.

"What's all this prove?" asked Mallory. "Can't say I wouldn't confess to every crime from tearin' down old man Johnson's fence to assassinatin' the president of these United States if that monster wrapped its nose around me and shook."

"Ask him again," Maddy urged.

Dellman was on hands and knees and looked up, terror etched on his wet face.

"Don't go sayin' a word, or you'll be diggin' your own grave," the sheriff told him. "You're guilty of something, but I just ain't figured out what yet. And I got to admit I got serious doubts about this bank robbery. Findin' that fancy watch layin' smack dab in the middle of the floor was real suspicious."

"If John was robbing the bank, he'd've done a better job," Maddy said. Slocum motioned for her to keep quiet. He didn't want the sheriff thinking he was more expert at robbery than the average citizen. The truth was he'd done more than one bank robbery in his day, both when he needed money and when he'd done it because the bank was an easy target.

"Little Al, anybody else been complain' about losin' their wallets or other valuables?"

"Only Mr. Wyatt, but he's always losing things," the deputy said.

"You do any other pickpocketing here in town?" Mallory pointed at Dellman, who bobbed his head up and down. Slocum wondered if Dellman was confessing to this or just wanting away from Trajan.

"We might stick together but there must have been town folk who saw Slocum during the performance. It must have taken a spell to break into the bank's safe." Maddy kept working at logical reasons to let Slocum go free.

Mallory snorted in disgust. "A blind man could have opened that safe. Been tellin' Prescott to get a real vault instead of that toy he used, but he's too much of a skinflint. Now he don't have much choice."

"But people saw Slocum during the show, didn't they?" Maddy pressed.

"That's why I'm listenin' to this yahoo's confession, even pressed out of him like it is. My sister-in-law told me she saw you shoot a clay pipe out of Slocum's mouth and someone else said they saw him holdin' that high-strung stallion until you came into the ring, but nobody can say for sure how long he stayed." Mallory scratched his chin and studied Slocum. "I've seen my share of guilty men, and you're as guilty as sin, but of what I can't say."

"Tell him again, Dellman. Tell the sheriff about you and Wilkins." Maddy prodded him with her rifle barrel. Slocum wanted her to stop forcing the man to confess. If he'd come out with something that sounded spontaneous, it would do a world of good more than dragging every word from his lips.

"It's more'n just me and Wilkins, Sheriff," Dellman said. "We got our orders, and we was following them to the letter. We never go against his orders."

"And who might that be?"

Dellman opened his mouth just as the shot rang out. The mouth made gaping motions like a fish out of water. The man tumbled face down into the street, dead before he hit the ground.

13

"Dellman!"

Slocum wasn't sure who shouted the man's name. It might have been Maddy or Andre—or he might have cried out himself. The single bullet had caught Dellman square in the temple, bringing him down like a tall tree being felled by an expert lumberjack.

"Get down, dammit. Don't give that sneaky bushwhacker another target." Sheriff Mallory shoved Slocum to the ground and drew his pistol. His deputy swung around, his shotgun leveled in the most likely direction of fire. A second bullet cut the deputy down like a weed. Little Al's knees turned to rubber, and he collapsed in a heap, never knowing what happened to him.

Slocum rolled in the street and kept rolling as tiny dust devils sprang up around him. A damned good shot was trying to remove him permanently from the face of the earth, and staying alive was getting harder by the second. His hands closed on the stock of the deputy's scattergun, but his fingers couldn't find the double triggers. He smashed hard into the watering trough where Trajan still sucked noisily at the water. Grunting in pain at what might be cracked ribs, Slocum came to his knees and peered under the elephant. He didn't see any good target, though bullets still sang in his direction.

"Maddy, get down," he called. Slocum wasn't interested in the woman obeying. He saw she had already found a safe spot behind a water barrel. He wanted to pull the sniper's attention in the woman's direction so Slocum could get a shot.

The bushwhacker didn't take the bait. There was a deadly silence, interrupted only by the sheriff's harsh breathing. Slocum heard his heart hammering, but it stilled quickly as he stood up and worked his way around Trajan. The elephant provided a good shield, even if Andre didn't like it.

"Get the elephant back to the circus," Slocum called. "I don't want that shooting fool putting holes in Trajan's valuable hide." He didn't have to tell the animal's handler twice. Andre's heels kicked behind the elephant's big ears and steered Trajan back toward the baron's big circus tent.

Slocum looked sideways at Sheriff Mallory to be sure the man wasn't singling him out for picking up the deputy's shotgun. The sheriff seemed more interested in dusting himself off.

"Damned nuisance," the lawman muttered. "Damned hard to find a good deputy in these parts." He pushed the toe of his boot into the dead deputy's side and rolled the man over. The bullet had gone through his body, a clean shot.

Slocum was more interested in Dellman. A head shot was hard to make, even if the target was standing stock-still. Dellman had been shaking like a leaf after being squeezed by Trajan, and more than a touch of fear had kept the man jumping around. There weren't many marksmen who could make a shot like that.

Clay Wilkins was such a sharpshooter.

Slocum was glad to see that the sheriff had come to the same conclusion. "Let's go do some serious talkin' to that eyewitness over at the Sells Brothers Circus," Mallory said. "Didn't much like the way he was so eager to finger you, Slocum." Mallory looked at the scattergun in Slocum's grip, as if seeing it for the first time. He silently held out his hand. Slocum hesitated, then passed it over. Mallory took the shotgun and tucked it under his arm so it rested in the crook of his left elbow.

"Am I still your prisoner?"

Slocum got his answer when Mallory handed over the watch. Slocum took it and spun it around, looking at the engraving on the back. His brother's watch was more precious to him than the lives of everyone in Wisdom, Utah. Slocum would sooner die himself than lose this last slender memory of his brother and their life growing up in Georgia.

"Someone go ask around the circus for Wilkins," Mallory called. Two of the crowd that was slowly gathering to see what had happened rushed off.

"Is that smart, Sheriff? Warning Wilkins instead of going for him is—"

"I'm not risking anyone's life," Mallory said. "Didn't you hear the horse hightailin' it out of town? I'm just makin' sure we're after the right varmint."

Slocum had been too busy dodging bullets to hear any hoofbeats. And the dominating presence of Trajan kept thoughts of anything much smaller from intruding. Still, it made sense that Wilkins wouldn't risk his neck by staying around town. He had just killed two men, one of them the town's deputy. Small towns were notorious for getting revenge when one of their own was cut down, especially when it was a lawman. Dellman might be considered an unfortunate victim, but Little Al must have relatives in these parts and friends who'd track his killer to the ends of the earth.

"What are you going to do, Sheriff?" Maddy moved closer to Slocum. He was uneasy about being this close to her. Mallory was probably right about the bushwhacker leaving town, but Slocum didn't want to present too good a target if Wilkins had doubled back and was going to try to bluff it out at the circus—or come back for another attempt.

"I'm going to do the best tracking of my life," he said simply. He spun and went back into the town jail. Slocum heard Mallory rooting around inside his desk. It took several minutes for him to find what he was hunting and re-emerge.

"Gather 'round, everybody," Mallory shouted. "I need a half dozen men to go with me."

"A posse, Sheriff?" someone called out.

"What do you think, you dimwit?" Mallory snapped. "I've got the badges. You'll be deputized. Who's going with me to get Little Al's killer?"

"You payin' regular wages?"

"You stupid son of a bitch!" Mallory shouted, getting madder. "What's a man's life worth to you? Little Al was a *good* man. That's more'n I can say for the lot of you."

"I'll go with you, Sheriff," Slocum said, stepping forward. He stared at the tin star in the lawman's hand with distaste. Slocum had been on the wrong end of too many posses to ever want to put on a badge, even for a few hours. "Keep your badge and your money. The owlhoot who shot down Dellman wanted me, too. This is the only way I can convince you."

"I'm convinced, Slocum," Mallory said in a low voice so only Slocum heard. He eyed Slocum for a few seconds and then shook his head. "You're not the law-abiding type. I've seen dozens like you come through here. Some are buried out in the potter's field, and the rest just kept on movin' through. This isn't your fight now that I'm sure you didn't have anything to do with the robbery."

Slocum glanced over his shoulder at the crowd. They milled around, confused. Slocum had been thrown into their town jail because he had robbed the bank and now Mallory was offering him a badge. The people didn't understand, and that made them even edgier.

"You sons of bitches go home to your warm dinners. I'll bring back Little Al's killer."

The crowd grumbled and began dispersing. Mallory grabbed Slocum by the arm and swung him around, shoving him toward the jail. "Get in," the sheriff said.

"I thought I was—"

"Shut up, Slocum. I don't have time for this. You any kind of a tracker?" Mallory's eyes blazed with anger at the people of Wisdom for not rushing to his aid. "Little Al was an orphan, and I was about all the friend he had. Can't expect them to stick their scrawny necks out, I suppose, but I'm still pissed off at 'em. And I don't want you along unless you meant what you said."

"I meant it, but I don't want to wear a badge."

"We all got our problems. I don't much care if you want to ride along with your longjohns flappin' in the breeze." Mallory seemed pleased that Slocum would go along.

"What about me?" came Maddy's question. "I can shoot with the best. Let me get Wilkins in my sights and—"

"No!" Mallory roared. "I don't want no woman along slowin' us down."

"I can ride with any man," Maddy said, her own anger rising.

"Go on back and tell the baron what's happened. He'll need you for the next show. Otherwise the Sells brothers will take away some of the thunder. We wouldn't want that." Slocum didn't think this would keep her from doing anything foolish, but he had to try to keep her occupied with circus work.

Maddy was torn between her loyalty to Baron Fenstermacher and gunning down Wilkins.

"The circus needs you," Slocum said in a low voice. "The baron doesn't need me. If anything happens . . ."

"John, no. It won't."

"The trail's getting cold, Sheriff," Slocum said, reaching out and touching Maddy's cheek. She turned and kissed his fingers. He pulled back. This wasn't the time for such things. He grabbed his holster and six-shooter from the cabinet beside the sheriff's desk and strapped down. He pulled the Colt from the cross-draw holster a couple times to be sure the six-shooter was situated properly. Mallory was already outside. Slocum cast one last look at Maddy, then hurried after the lawman.

The trail was getting cold. The sooner they got Clay Wilkins the sooner Slocum would sleep easy.

"I swear that man's got more tricks up his sleeve than any Injun I ever saw," Mallory said, wiping the sweat from his forehead. "He couldn't've been more than a few minutes ahead of us, and here he is leavin' us farther back with every hour."

Slocum had to agree that the man they tracked was more ghost than human. The night had been brightened by a sliver of a moon, and Slocum had been able to find the trail without much trouble. But the man leaving it had consistently laid false leads, turned and twisted, sent them on wild goose chases, and had eluded them with an ease that bespoke of long practice.

"You have any idea where we are?" Slocum looked around and wasn't sure where they'd ended up. He thought Wisdom was just over a low, razor-backed ridge, their tracking bringing them almost full circle, but he couldn't be sure.

"That there's a spur from the railroad," Mallory said. "Looks like there's a train movin' along the tracks, slowlike. Must be the second train you said you were expecting to show up. And back there is—" Mallory never finished his sentence. The shot echoed through the night and took him from the saddle.

Slocum whipped his rifle from its saddle sheath but had no idea where the shot had come from. He slipped from the back of his sorrel and sidled toward the fallen lawman. Mallory groaned and cursed. Slocum knew he wasn't wounded too badly.

"Got me in the side. Damn him! If I could shoot half as good, I'd give up being sheriff and do nothing but hunt all year. Damn, but this hurts." Mallory sat up and held his side. Slocum saw dark blood oozing between the man's fingers.

"You'd better get on back to town and let a sawbones work on you."

"I'm not hurt that bad. From where the bullet struck, that backshooter's got to be out there. If he is, we got him by the balls."

"Why?" Slocum asked. "There something in that direction worth mentioning?"

"Surely is," Mallory said, struggling to his feet. "A box canyon. We got him trapped unless he can turn into a bird and fly out. There's no kid in Wisdom that can make it up the cliff at the end of Square Canyon in less than a day. At night?" Mallory shook his head. "We got him penned-up good."

"The only difference is that the kids don't shoot back," Slocum said, watching the lawman carefully. The painful way Mallory mounted his horse told of a wound worse than he let on. His pride had been damaged back in town when no one volunteered to join the posse. Slocum wasn't sure Mallory had been that much of a friend to Little Al, no matter what the lawman claimed, but the sheriff couldn't let the death go unavenged.

"It's two of us against one of him. Just don't go silhouetting yourself so he can potshot you," Mallory warned. "The moon don't look like much, but it's enough to make you shine like you're wearin' polished silver."

Slocum would take that advice, if he could figure out where Wilkins might be. They rode forward slowly, Slocum laying his Winchester across the saddle in front of him. He was a good shot but he had to have a target before he opened up.

He saw the foot-long tongue of flame from the rifle before he heard the report. Slocum lifted his Winchester and returned fire almost before the bullet whined past his ear. He had come within inches of having his head blown off.

"Got 'im, Slocum. I see 'im!" Mallory opened up from a few yards off. Slocum and the sheriff pumped round after round into the mouth of the canyon, but Slocum had the feeling they weren't doing much good.

He jumped when another rifle fired twenty yards to his right. The sheriff was to his left and their quarry was in front.

"It's me, John. I see him." Madeleine Scowcroft fired with measured accuracy, but Slocum wasn't sure she was doing any better a job than he was. There had to be a target before you could hit it. He had the gut feeling that Wilkins had slipped away.

"What are you doing out here?" demanded Mallory. The sheriff rode over. Slocum saw him clutching his side. The dark spot had spread, showing the wound was worse than Mallory admitted.

"You didn't wait for the men to report back, Sheriff."

"What men are you talking about?"

"The two you sent to check on Clay Wilkins." Maddy's voice took on a brittle tone that warned Slocum he wasn't going to like what she was going to say.

"What happened?" Slocum asked.

"Wilkins was putting on a show, him and Billy. He was putting on a demonstration of fancy shooting for some town folk. And he had been there most of the night after telling the sheriff you'd robbed the bank."

"I don't understand," Mallory said.

"It's simple enough, Sheriff," Slocum said, staring into the darkness. "Whoever we have bottled up in that box canyon of yours isn't Clay Wilkins."

14

Slocum scratched his head and frowned. They were after someone who was damned good at evasion. Even considering they were after the man in the dark, their quarry was giving them a hell of a time. It certainly explained a great deal, Slocum thought. He had pegged Clay Wilkins as a blowhard and not half the man he thought he was. Someone so full of himself wouldn't be skilled in hiding a trail, though Slocum had to admit Wilkins was passing good when it came to being a sharpshooter.

"Don't matter none," Mallory said. "Whoever we got holed up in Square Canyon shot Dellman and Little Al. A murderer's a murderer, and I want him to swing for it."

Slocum saw how the sheriff tottered in the saddle. It wouldn't take more than a gentle breeze to knock the man off his mount. He reached over and gripped the lawman's shoulder and was startled by how cold the flesh was.

"What you tryin' to do to me, Slocum?" Mallory gripped the saddlehorn with both hands to keep himself upright. "There's nothing wrong with me. I been wounded worse than this before."

"Let me take a look at it," Slocum said. "It won't hurt to get it bound up."

"Yes, Sheriff," chimed in Maddy. "You said this is a box

canyon. We've got him trapped."

"It's a box canyon, but there's a trail up the back all the way to the rim. Ain't much of a canyon."

"The wound," Slocum said.

"We ride. You get on back to the circus, Miss Scowcroft. This ain't no place for a woman."

"She's good with a rifle," Slocum said. "Better 'n most men."

"There might be some killin'," Mallory said, sitting straighter now. "And I don't want you gettin' ventilated like I've been."

"Go on back, Maddy," Slocum said. He bent close and whispered in her ear, "Follow close and keep your rifle ready. This is going to be bloody." By now the man they chased had found out he had ridden into a trap. He didn't seem to be the kind to just give up without a fight, not when he was so deadly accurate.

"All right," she said with the proper amount of regret in her voice. She looked from Slocum to the sheriff and back. "You take care and watch your back." She swung her white stallion's head and galloped off for several minutes. Slocum waited until the sound of the hoofbeats died down. Straining, he caught the sound of a slower return as she walked her horse back. He wasn't sure this was the right thing to do; the sheriff was right that this could turn deadly in a flash, and having Maddy in the middle of it wasn't right. The highwayman who had waylaid them had been the first man she'd ever killed.

"What you waitin' for, Slocum? Getting cold feet?"

"No, just worried about you," Slocum said. It occurred to him that Mallory had figured out what had happened in town, but only the dead deputy knew that Slocum had no part in the bank robbery. That left a powerful lot of explaining to do if Mallory didn't make it back.

"Keep close. There's no need to go ridin' apart," Mallory told him. "The trail into the canyon don't amount to much, but—" He didn't get a chance to finish. The bullet ripping through the still of the night took off the sheriff's hat and sent it spinning.

Slocum wasn't sure if Mallory had been hit by the way he flopped off his horse and crashed to the ground.

"Get down, you fool," called Mallory. "You're a sittin' duck up there. He's got you silhouetted!"

The second bullet was meant for Slocum, but he was already bending low and getting out of the way. His sorrel reared but he kept it under control. When the animal's initial panic had passed, Slocum slipped down the side, keeping the horse between him and the bushwhacker. Even assuming Mallory was right and that they had committed a greenhorn's error of outlining themselves against the sky, someone was doing damned good shooting.

Slocum got his Winchester free of its scabbard and dropped beside the sheriff. He said nothing as he scanned the cliff to their left where the shots had come from. He heard Mallory's labored breathing and knew the strain was taking its toll on the man's endurance. The bleeding hadn't stopped, either. Before they could tend to the wound, though, they had to get free of the sniper.

"He's about halfway up the side of the canyon," Mallory said. "I saw the muzzle flash when he took his shot at you."

"Where?"

Mallory rolled over and came to rest beside Slocum. The effort made the man pant harshly. Sweat beaded on his forehead in spite of the cold wind whipping out of the canyon's mouth. Slocum had to look twice to be sure it was sweat and not more blood.

"Up there. See the round spot? That's a cave entrance. Not deep enough to be exciting for the town kids, but it'd make a fine place to ambush us."

"He must have rode hard to find this was a box canyon and get all the way back here," Slocum said. Or maybe the sharpshooter trying to get them in his sights had never entered the canyon and had just laid a trap for them.

"He's a tricky one, I'll grant you that," Mallory said. There was a wheezing now to his words that Slocum had heard before. Men sounded like this just before they upped and died.

Slocum squeezed off a shot that hit the center of the darkness Mallory had identified. The bullet ricocheted around in the shallow depression. Slocum smiled when he heard cursing. There wasn't any way he could have hoped for a hit, but the flying lead was doing the trick. He fired again, then started moving to get closer. If he could trap the man they hunted on the side of the cliff, he'd have to surrender or get cut down trying to reach the top—Slocum would have cut him off from his horse, which must have been left somewhere on the canyon floor.

"There!" shouted Mallory. "See?"

Slocum blinked at the flash of the other's rifle. He had a target now and began firing quickly. He was rewarded with more cursing from the side of the canyon. He didn't have a feel that he had hit the man, but their quarry knew now he was in for a fight.

"Go get 'im. I'll cover you," Mallory said eagerly.

Slocum took time to reload, then sprinted for cover at the bottom of the cliff. Looking up didn't give him any target. All he saw was rock outcropping, but the man overhead didn't have a good shot at him, either. Slocum edged along the face of the cliff, waiting for a chance. If he came across the man's horse, the chase was over. They could run down a man on foot without much trouble.

Rock tumbled from above. Slocum moved away and looked up. He took a quick shot at what he thought was the man. He had made a mistake and got answering fire from a completely different location. Cursing his buck fever, Slocum dashed to the cliff and pressed his back against the cold rock. They were in the middle of a Mexican standoff unless something changed the odds.

Two quick shots from Mallory changed everything. Slocum heard a gasp as the man above him in the rocks was hit. It wasn't much, he decided, but it'd slow him down.

Slocum looked for a way up when he heard Maddy call out, "John, the sheriff's hurt bad."

He paused, wondering if this was a trick to draw out the sniper above him. But she called again. He heard the panic in her voice and knew he had to make a decision. The sheriff could clear him—if he got Mallory back to town before he died.

Bringing in the man in the rocks wouldn't do anything but make Slocum feel better. There might not be enough evidence to convict him of Dellman's murder without the sheriff's testimony.

Slocum hated doing it but he darted from bush to bush, ducking down an arroyo to cover the final few yards to where Maddy knelt by the sheriff. Her face was pale and strained.

"It's bad, John. He took another bullet. The first one was bad, but this one . . ." She pulled away the sheriff's shirt to show how much blood he was losing.

Slocum glanced back at the canyon wall and heaved a deep sigh. He wanted the backshooting owlhoot up there, but he had to tend to the sheriff first.

"Help get him onto his horse," Slocum said, heaving Mallory over his shoulder. He might have imagined it but Slocum thought he heard mocking laughter rolling out of the canyon.

"Is he going to make it?" Maddy chewed her lower lip as she studied Sheriff Mallory's limp form. Slocum rode closer and bent over, putting his finger under the lawman's nose.

"There's still breathing going on," he said, "but it's getting weaker."

"Maybe you should let me take him on into town," she said. "He's the only one who can clear you for certain. Everyone else is dead or not going to speak up."

"I'll stay with him," Slocum said. He knew it would be worse if he hightailed it now. If the sheriff did die without exonerating him, he'd be wanted for murdering a lawman as well as bank robbery. It might not have been Clay Wilkins who had framed him, but whoever it was couldn't be allowed to win that easily. Slocum had to stick this one out and do what was right.

"There're the town lights," Madeleine said, pointing. "We'll make it. I'm sure of it."

Slocum only grunted. He knew she was trying to bolster

his flagging spirits. He didn't need anything but a few minutes with the bushwhacker who had shot the sheriff—and
who had framed him. Wilkins was mixed up in the scheme
up to his earlobes, and Slocum knew that the sharpshooter
was where he had to start. But he needed Mallory alive for
a while longer if he wanted to be able to show his face
without the other deputy shooting it off.

"Ride on ahead and find a doctor. Mallory didn't have
good things to say for the local sawbones, but he's our only
chance."

"I can get Doc Poussard."

"Who's that?"

"The circus vet. He knows everything about animals
and patches us up when we get banged around out on
the road."

"Get him first, then find the town doctor," Slocum decided. He had more faith in a bad veterinarian than he did in
a good doctor. For one thing, their bedside manner was
better.

"Where will you be?" Madeleine asked.

"The jail. Can't think of anywhere else to meet, and the
cot in the back looks to be where Mallory sleeps. Don't
know if he has a permanent place to hang his hat or not."

"All right, John. Take care." She blinked back tears
and looked as if she might ride closer to kiss him, but
she didn't. Maddy turned her horse and put spurs to the
stallion's powerful sides. The horse galloped off, a white
smear across the darkness of night. Slocum kept riding at
a slower pace, not wanting to bounce Mallory too much.

He got to the jail about the same time as the town
doctor. Poussard was already waiting. Slocum had seen
the man but had never connected his activity with being
a vet. Poussard seemed to be a jack-of-all-trades with the
circus, but the small black bag he had with him identified
him as a medical man.

"Is this the patient?" Poussard helped Slocum get the
sheriff off the horse and into the office, where they laid
him gently on the sagging cot.

"He took two bullets in the side. The first one might

not be too bad, but it bled like hell. The second one . . ." Slocum shook his head to show he wasn't sure Mallory would survive.

Poussard ripped open the sheriff's shirt and probed. Mallory complained, trying to pull away. It was the first hint Slocum had that the lawman was still alive since he'd checked out on the trail.

"What's going on?" Lucas, the sometime deputy, barged in. He had three men trailing behind like captives. From outside came a squawk of anger. The men parted and let a smallish man dressed in black enter. From his bloodshot eyes and shaking hands, he was drunker than a skunk. Slocum didn't have to be told who the town doctor was.

"Lemme see him," the doctor said. Poussard was already working to get the bullets out of Mallory. Slocum moved slightly so the doctor crashed into him and recoiled.

"Out of my way, you lout," the doctor cried.

Slocum looked at Lucas. The deputy swallowed hard, then took the doctor's arm and guided him to a chair at the other side of the office. Whatever he said to the doctor cooled the man off, and he went diving immediately into his bag for a small flask. He knocked back a good slug of the whiskey and sat contentedly.

"He's not much but he's all we got. This your doc?" Lucas pointed at Poussard.

"Fixes up everyone at the circus," Slocum said, glossing over Poussard's real job. "Never can tell when a man's likely to break an arm falling from a highwire or burn himself eating fire."

"And those animals," Lucas said. "They look real mean. They could tear a man up."

"Haven't had much call for that kind of patch work," Poussard said. "Mostly, it's the other way, trying to fix what men do to the animals." He pushed back, his hands and arms covered with blood. "That's all I can do. A bit of whiskey sloshed into the wounds might help."

It took Lucas a few seconds to pry the flask loose from the doctor. Mallory winced as the liquor burned his two bullet wounds.

The sheriff's eyes blinked open. "Thanks, Slocum, you saved me."

"Tell them, Sheriff, tell them I'm not a suspect."

"You? Hell, no, not a suspect. Bushwhacker what got me robbed the bank. Only way to figure it out. Slocum and me hunted him down but he winged me."

"It was either bring the sheriff back and let the owlhoot go or stay and maybe see him die," Slocum said, wanting to be sure Lucas understood. The deputy wasn't too bright but he got the idea.

"Reckon you're a free man, Slocum," Lucas finally said. "The town of Wisdom owes you a debt for saving the sheriff like you did."

"All I want is for the man who gunned him down to be brought to justice," Slocum said. "You can start by questioning Clay Wilkins."

"Wilkins? That fellow with the Sells Brothers Circus?"

"What's wrong?"

"Their entire circus done pulled out more'n an hour ago. There was some kind of argument over at the railroad yard, but they got it worked out. Your train's waitin', and they took theirs on, or so they said. I'd need more'n suspicion to telegraph ahead and have the law down the line hold him."

Slocum rested his hand on the butt of his Colt Navy. Wilkins might have slipped free this time, but the railroad still went only in one direction, and the baron's circus would be rolling along the next day. Then it would be time to settle accounts.

15

"It is a disaster what they have done to us," moaned Baron Fenstermacher. The man fiddled with his mustache until the ends turned fuzzy and tried to look as if he wasn't going to break down crying at any instant. Slocum didn't think he did too good a job. The man's lip quivered and set the tips of his poorly waxed mustache to wiggling like caterpillars on a hot rock.

"What now?" Slocum asked. He was dog tired and wasn't in any mood to deal with business problems Kincaid would have handled. He and Poussard had spent most of the night and early morning with Sheriff Mallory to be sure his care wasn't going to be handed over to the lush of a town doctor. The lawman had drifted into a shallow sleep, but Poussard had declared him fit enough to survive. That was all right with Slocum, though he had seldom met an officer of the law he much liked. He had no quarrel with Mallory, and the man had been honest and even diligent about his job rather than trying to pin the bank robbery on the most likely suspect, which had been Slocum.

"The railroad, always the railroad," moaned the baron. He sat heavily, plopping down in the mud from watering Trajan and the other animals. He put his forehead in his

131

hands and actually wept. Slocum had no time for such a show of emotion in a man.

"John, don't think harshly of him. He's not like us. He's—" Madeleine tried to put it into words. Dr. Poussard finished her thought for her.

"He is European. We take such setbacks hard."

Slocum tried not to show his contempt. If there was a problem, you didn't sit around like a bunch of old women crying about it. You went out and did something about what was wrong. And then you either corrected it or you didn't. Either way, you didn't bawl your eyes out.

"What about the train?" he asked Madeleine. She seemed to have some idea what was causing the baron's upset.

"The other circus pulled out early."

"I know. The deputy told us Wilkins and the others had left on their train a couple hours before we got back. All that means is that they're on their own train again and we've got ours." Slocum peered into the bright sunlight and saw the old engine and the line of cars behind it. The piston had been fixed, and the crew lounged around waiting for the baron to order the freight cars loaded.

"It's more complicated than that, John. There's the matter of the bill."

"The circus did well here. The baron said so."

"It's Wilkins, damn his soul," flared Maddy. "He stuck us with the bill for both trains. The baron paid—and Wilkins and the rest of the Sells Brothers Circus got on the train and went off. Now *our* engineer wants payment, and we don't have it."

Slocum ran his hand through his lank black hair. He ought to get on his horse and ride, it didn't matter what direction. The baron wasn't paying him enough for this kind of frustration. Fact was, he hadn't collected a single paycheck from the baron since he'd been with the circus. Slocum didn't understand what kind of businessman Fenstermacher was to pay a bill owed by another company. Kincaid couldn't have run the circus so completely that the owner had no idea what was going on financially.

"He didn't understand, John. He speaks good English but he didn't grasp what Wilkins was doing."

Slocum listened and heard the animals in their cages stirring, roaring, trumpeting, bellowing, making odd noises—and he heard their handlers speaking a half-dozen different languages. This was truly a Continental circus. Andre was French, as was the veterinarian. The baron was German, Morelli Italian, and the rest of the performers were from countries Slocum had hardly heard of. A sharp character like Wilkins could almost always put something over on them if he spoke fast enough, and he didn't doubt the engineer of the train carrying the rival circus had had a part in the fraud, too.

Being paid twice was the sort of thing any dishonest man would jump at, especially since there was little likelihood of being caught for the double charging.

"I'll talk to the engineer," Slocum said.

"It is no use. He will not relent. He is of cast iron. We are ruined!"

Slocum ignored the baron's cries and walked toward the engineer. The furtive look in the railroad man's eyes told Slocum this might be a conspiracy between both engineers and Wilkins to fleece the baron. Before the engineer could turn tail and run, Slocum pinned him against the side of his engine.

"We need to get on down the line," he said, his face less than an inch from the engineer's. He smelled liquor on the man's breath and saw real fear mounting in the piglike eyes.

"Can't do it. You got to pay what you owe."

"If you don't take the circus to the next town, you won't collect a dime," Slocum pointed out. "Would you rather turn around and go home with your tail between your legs or would you rather try to collect what's due you?"

"It costs money to run a steam engine. I can't—"

"Where'd you get the whiskey?" Slocum asked. "Did Wilkins give it to you? Or maybe it was the other engineer."

"Their conductor," the frightened man blurted. He turned pale when he realized that he was confessing to a conspiracy. "I ain't done nothing wrong. Honest."

"You don't know the meaning of the word honest," Slocum said, "but you're going to take Baron Fenstermacher's Fabulous Continental Circus all the way to the next stop before demanding payment. Aren't you?"

"You can't threaten me." The engineer showed some spunk. Slocum hated spunk.

"I'm not threatening you. I'm asking for a favor which you, as a decent, honest man, will grant us. Otherwise, there's no telling what might happen."

"What do you mean?"

"*I'd* never harm you, but the baron's damned near crazy with grief, and you heard what he did the last time he snapped." Slocum tapped the side of his head.

"What?" The engineer trembled openly now.

"The lions. He feeds people to the lions—feet first. Takes longer for the lion to eat them that way, and they know what's happening up till the knees or so. You remember his former business manager Kincaid?"

"The lions?"

"Old Leo had company in his cage. Ask anyone."

"I heard something about it," the man admitted. "I didn't believe it. Rumors . . ."

"All true. How long before you can be ready to get up a head of steam?"

"F-forty-five minutes," the man stuttered.

"That's convenient," Slocum said, moving back from the man. "That's about how long it'll take to get the equipment and animals loaded."

If he had planned it, the timing couldn't have been better. Simba and Leo began roaring loudly. The engineer took off as if he'd been shot out of a cannon.

Slocum returned to where the baron had picked himself up and was looking regal again, chin up, and dignity restored except for his muddy britches.

"Get to work," Slocum said. "The engineer's agreed to wait until the next town for payment."

"He has?" Baron Fenstermacher was shocked, then smiled broadly. "But of course he will wait. He knows we will be a success there!"

The baron rushed off to get the roustabouts working. Maddy looked at Slocum and shook her head in wonder.

"Don't ask," Slocum said. "But I'd advise you to tell the handlers to keep the lions roaring as loud as they can until we're moving."

"It won't be easy," Maddy said. "The Sells brothers are already on the way. Having the same schedule is killing us. They'll milk the next town of every cent and—"

"So skip it and go straight on to the next. Leapfrog them," Slocum said in exasperation.

"I want Wilkins," she said, a flush coming to her pale cheeks. "I want him so bad I can taste it."

For once he had run into an argument that overrode common sense. He wanted Wilkins, too—and the unknown man who had framed him for bank robbery.

"It's going to be tight," Maddy said. "They got here first, and I have to hand it to them, they put on a good parade. It draws the audience like flies to honey."

"There's a matter of money paid to the other engineer," Slocum said. "I'm going to collect it."

Maddy held him back. "John, did you ever stop to think this might be what Wilkins wants? He's tried throwing us in jail, framing you, every dirty trick possible. He might want the engineer to file charges against you. The baron can't afford to lose you." She looked up at him, her ebony eyes bottomless. "I can't stand to lose you, either."

Slocum wondered about her intentions. She had been alternately distant and close, hot and cold. He couldn't understand what it was eating at her.

"What do you want to do?"

"I'm primed and ready to have another shootout with Wilkins. You and me against him and the boy."

Slocum almost laughed. "Billy's damned good, maybe better than I am."

"He's good but he's not as good as you, now that you know what you're up against. And I know I can outshoot Clay Wilkins. I know it!"

"I've got a few dollars for a wager," Slocum said. "If nothing else, it'll bring the baron's circus to the attention of the crowd Wilkins has already drawn." At the far end of the street Slocum saw where the Bogardus Shooting Team was putting on a demonstration of its skills. Without Dellman the task fell heavily on young Billy while Wilkins worked the crowd.

"I want to show him up, John. I do. And I will." The determination told him she'd die trying to best Wilkins. Slocum worried about their last meeting, and how he had the gut feeling Wilkins had somehow cheated. He didn't want to get into another match without knowing how.

Slocum inclined his head in the direction of the Sells Brothers Circus and off they went. The crowd was ten deep around Billy, forcing Slocum and Maddy to elbow their way to the front. A few made rude remarks, but Slocum ignored them.

Billy laid down a rifle with a red-hot barrel from rapid shooting and took up another when he saw Slocum. A shy smile crossed the boy's face, and he nodded greeting.

Wilkins saw instantly and spun around. Before he could speak, Maddy cried out, "We're here to challenge you to a shoot-out. The pair of us against you two. Any stakes you want."

Slocum tried to stop her from the wild challenge, but she had already spoken. He had forty or fifty dollars in his pocket, and that was all. From everything that had happened, the baron probably didn't have that much. A real wager was out of the question.

"Any stakes?" called Wilkins in a loud voice. "Any at all?"

"Keep it reasonable," Slocum said, trying to head off what he saw was coming. The Bogardus Shooting Team had resources he and Maddy lacked.

"One thousand dollars is a reasonable sum," shouted Wilkins. "Or do you want to back down?"

"Maddy," Slocum started, but the woman pulled free and stepped forward.

"We accept!"

A roar went up from the crowd. Such a fantastic sum bet on a shoot-out was unheard of in Utah. Slocum wondered if Maddy was out of her mind. There was no way in hell they could pay such a phenomenal sum if they lost.

And Wilkins had a way of cheating. That kept nagging Slocum.

"How do you want to do it? The highest number of consecutive hits?" suggested Wilkins.

"The best score out of a thousand targets," countered Maddy. "Each member of either team will get five hundred shots."

"We need someone to do the counting," Slocum said.

"I couldn't agree more," cut in Wilkins. "There, there's just the gentleman for our match. Please, Reverend, step forward."

A man dressed in a severely cut black broadcloth suit and carrying a Bible under his arm hesitated, then came through the crowd to stand by the table holding a half-dozen rifles.

"What do you want of me, my son?"

"Just count, that's all, Reverend. Is this satisfactory?"

Slocum started to protest but Maddy cut him off. "Let's get down to shooting." She placed her own ammunition on the table and hefted her rifle with the silver dollars embedded in the stock. "We'll show you that the crack team from Baron Fenstermacher's Fabulous Continental Circus can outshoot, outride, and out-circus anyone west of the Mississippi."

Slocum liked the way she told the crowd who they worked for, but he felt he was being railroaded. He placed his rifle on the table and shucked off his coat. The day was already hot and was going to get a mite hotter.

"You surely do shoot up a storm," Billy said shyly. "Don't see too many as good as you." He almost blushed when he added, "Or Miss Scowcroft."

"May the best team win," Slocum said, thrusting his hand out for Billy to shake. He didn't repeat the offer to Wilkins, and this seemed to please the boy as much as hitting one hundred straight targets.

They began shooting and within ten minutes found a problem. No single man could toss the targets fast enough. Slocum and Maddy agreed to allow a random selection from the crowd to do the throwing, relying on the minister to keep an honest count since some threw higher and slower than others.

Slocum occasionally took a look at how Wilkins and Billy were doing. Billy shot with mechanical skill, missing only one or two that Slocum saw. Wilkins fired with less precision but seemed to have a better record. Slocum rubbed his sore shoulder and gave his rifle barrel a long rest and watched Maddy working.

Her jaw was set with grim determination, and she didn't miss a single target. The ground was littered with glass shards and what just amount to ten pounds of feathers. If pure guts could win the day, Madeleine Scowcroft was a sure winner.

Slocum glanced over the reverend's shoulder at the score pad and then frowned. The count was way off. He hadn't missed a single target and yet he was shown as missing two. And Slocum had seen Billy miss a pair, one after the other and his score was a perfect ninety-eight.

"Wait," he said. "There's something wrong with the count."

"Nonsense. I am doing—"

"The count is wrong," Slocum insisted.

"I been counting," chimed in someone from the crowd. A second and third also shouted they had been keeping track of the targets thrown and missed.

"Write down your scores," Slocum said. "I want to compare with the preacher man."

"I got you two hitting two-oh-eight out of two-ten. Damned good shooting. And they got two hundred even out of two-oh-two." A grizzled old man in the crowd came up with the figures. He looked to be a prospector just in from a long search for gold, but everyone seemed to know him. Others agreed with his figures. But the preacher protested loudly.

The argument ebbed and flowed and finally those were the numbers agreed on, the preacher's count changed. Slocum could hardly believe it, though enough in the town agreed. Billy had missed the only two targets for the Bogardus team. Wilkins was proving to be a better shot—or a cleverer sneak—than Slocum had thought.

"Let's keep shooting," Slocum said. "We got another hour to go before they can catch up." He got a laugh from the audience, which was what he wanted. He had to keep them interested enough to keep an honest tally. Firing methodically, he broke eighty more targets before missing. And he heard Maddy's rifle barking out an even faster pace.

"That there's five hundred each," came the cry just before sundown. Slocum was seeing double and his shoulder was heavily bruised from the constant firing. He wasn't sure his Winchester would ever be the same, either, its barrel getting so hot that it was slightly askew.

The count was in dispute, the townspeople arguing among themselves as to which team had won.

"We won," cried Wilkins. "The Bogardus Shooting Team has won!"

"Not so fast," Slocum said. "Let them get it straight among themselves."

"I want my money. One thousand dollars," insisted Wilkins.

"We can't decide," a grizzled old man said. "And that preacher fellow is getting us all confused. Who the hell is he, anyhow?"

"What's that?" asked Slocum. "He's your minister, isn't he?"

"Him? We never saw him 'fore today. Most all of us are Mormons. Ain't no other church in town. Whatever he is, he ain't no saint."

Slocum spun on Wilkins, fire in his eye. "You paying him to lie for you?"

"Never saw him before," Wilkins lied, and Slocum knew it was a whopper. "Settle the bet."

"He was cheating," Slocum said. "I want you all to tell us who won."

"John, wait." Maddy put her hand on his arm. The hand was sweaty from clutching the rifle all afternoon. "They might decide against us."

After a few minutes, the old man said, "We can't agree. Either you won by three or *they* won by two. That's as close as we can come. Fact is, we was watching the fancy shootin' more than counting."

"Then it's a draw," boomed Baron Fenstermacher's rumbling bass. "A fine spectacle this was, but there's an even better one waiting for you under the big top. Come one, come all, enjoy a true Continental circus performance this evening!"

Baron Fenstermacher began handing out flyers and free tickets to a few of the boys in the young crowd.

Before Wilkins could begin his spiel, Slocum stopped him and said, "You were cheating."

"The preacher? I don't know who he was. I was taken in just like you."

"There's something else, Wilkins. I'm going to find out how you shot a perfect five hundred this afternoon."

Clay Wilkins jerked free of Slocum's grip and gathered his rifles. He snarled at Billy and the two went inside their tent and left the baron to his own devices. Within minutes the baron had a sizable crowd following him back to his circus for a show.

Slocum watched the crowd leave. His shoulder ached, and he knew Wilkins had cheated. And he was going to find out how.

16

"We could have done better," Maddy said, watching as the crowd slowly left the tent after the last performance. "Trajan was the real hit of the show, as usual." She let out a sigh that Slocum took to mean she wished she was the headliner that pulled the crowds.

"Nobody knows how hard it is doing the kind of shooting you do every performance," Slocum said. He rotated his shoulder and wondered how Maddy kept from getting stiff from such omnibus shooting. Five hundred rounds was only half what the long matches ran, and Maddy had told him of exhibitions Carver and Bogardus had given where they had shot at ten thousand over a week's span. After the first few rounds, it became an endurance contest rather than a trial of marksmanship.

"You're too kind," she said. "Still, all Trajan does is look big. He didn't practice to be such an attraction."

"And he didn't train his horse to do what yours does," Slocum said. Maddy smiled almost shyly at the memory of her stallion trotting around the ring and the two of them on its back.

"You look tuckered out, John. Would you like me to wash your back?"

"Soaking my shoulder is more important," he said honestly. His left arm was almost numb from the pounding of the rifle butt against it a few hours earlier.

"It takes getting used to," she said, "and I always pad my shirts." She turned to show him. Slocum wasn't looking at the thin cotton but instead at how her fringed vest had come open.

"Reckon so," he said. Maddy hadn't noticed his interest. He couldn't figure her out. At times she was hotter than a two-dollar pistol, and at other times she was oblivious to everything around her. The circus and being a sharpshooter were central to her life, Slocum knew. If she hadn't been good at shooting, she would have found something else to do so she could be in front of the crowds, seeking their approval through applause. To Slocum this was a limited kind of regard and not worth a great deal.

"I should see if the baron needs any help," Slocum said.

"He's doing just fine. We hadn't thought to make a dime here, and the gate was good. The shoot-out took a considerable crowd away from the Sells Brothers Circus. They're going to have to think about keeping the Bogardus Shooting Team as part of their show."

"They could just get rid of Wilkins," Slocum said, following her from the tent into the cold night. Altitude had given the summer wind an edge like steel. He wished he had his duster to hold back some of the chill.

"Bracing out tonight, isn't it?" she said, not seeming to notice the cold at all. She was bare-armed, and the way her vest hung open even more, Slocum hoped she didn't get a chest cold. "Let's go for a walk."

They walked through the town, which was slowly going to sleep. When they reached the far end and the other circus, they were surrounded by almost complete silence and darkness.

"The moon's just sneaking up. It's almost full tonight," she said. "I remember walking with Joseph on nights like this. It seems so long ago."

"An hour or a lifetime can seem short, depending on how you think," Slocum said. He put his arm around her, but she picked up the pace and kept a little in front of him. They walked in silence a while longer until Maddy suddenly stopped.

"Did you hear it?"

"The crunching?" Slocum glanced down at the ground. Silver moonlight shone off the broken targets the four of them had spent the afternoon breaking. The feathers had been blown away by the wind, except a few impaled on spiny cactuses.

"There's something wrong," she said, kneeling. "Wilkins shot too good. Even with the fake preacher cheating on his behalf, Wilkins shot too good. There's got to be a reason."

"I've been thinking on this," Slocum said, an idea finally forming. "He was trying to use cracked targets the first time we had a match."

"Bogardus manufactures the targets," Maddy said. "That's no surprise that some of them would be defective."

"Wilkins always seemed to get those," Slocum said, "but I called him on it, and he stopped. I checked to be sure, but I never checked his ammunition."

"I saw the boxes on the table. They looked like regular .44-40 rounds, the kind Bogardus prefers."

"Did each report sound right to you?"

"What are you getting at?" Maddy frowned and began digging through the desert. She filtered sand, glass, and lead between her fingers, letting it all fall back to the ground. She took another handful and then stopped, examining a tiny pellet in the palm of her hand. Looking up, a mask of anger formed on her lovely face.

"He pulled some powder out of the cartridges," Slocum said, "and filled the gap with birdshot."

"This is the proof," Maddy said, holding her hand out. Slocum took the tiny birdshot pellet and rolled it between his fingers. It was hardly big enough to break a glass target, but if the .44 slug didn't completely do the job, the cloud of lighter shot would finish. Wilkins could miss by fractions and still make a clean target break.

"He's one low-down snake, that's for sure," Slocum said. "We can't prove it, though. This might have been out here for months. Some kid from town might have gone bird hunting. Even if we find five pounds of birdshot, there's no way of proving it."

"We *did* outshoot him, by damn," Maddy said angrily. "We won, and he weaseled out of it!"

Slocum said nothing. He hadn't liked the way Maddy had committed a thousand dollars of money they didn't have to the match, and now it appeared even more foolhardy. Clay Wilkins had rigged the match.

"There's something else to consider," Slocum said. "Who was it who shot Dellman and robbed the bank back in Wisdom?"

"What difference does it make?"

Slocum couldn't forget the bullets winging through the night, seeking his body with such deadly accuracy. Wilkins did everything he could to stack the deck in his favor. Whoever had been shooting with such skill hadn't needed the small cheats Wilkins used.

"Next time we know what else to inspect," Slocum said. "Maybe we can switch ammo on him. That ought to put him into a pretty pickle."

"I want more than just beating him, John. I want to kill that son of a bitch for all he's done. He's trying to ruin the baron!"

"Why?" Slocum asked. "What does Wilkins have against him?"

"Why, I—" For a moment Maddy was speechless. "I don't know. It must be that I'm a better sharpshooter than he is, and he wants to destroy the baron because of it."

"There's got to be more reason than that," Slocum said. He wondered if the mystery gunman might not come into the dilemma.

Maddy threw her handful of shot and sand to the ground and spun around, facing away, arms crossed tightly over her chest. From this angle Slocum thought she had turned to quicksilver. Her pale skin shone like metal and her dark hair almost vanished except when a sharp breeze carried some of the lustrous hair away from her face like a small banner flapping in the wind.

He put his arms around her, and this time she didn't pull away. She leaned back, her head resting on his left shoulder. Slocum tried not to wince at even this slight pressure.

"I don't know what I want any more, John. I used to be happy with Baron Fenstermacher. The circus gave me a home when Joseph died and has been more of a family for me than any other I've known."

Slocum didn't know how to answer the woman. She was working over deep problems he couldn't begin to guess. He turned her in his arms and looked down into her moonlit face. Her dark eyes looked like pools of molten fire. He kissed her.

For a moment Maddy didn't respond, then the outpouring of passion almost overwhelmed Slocum. Again he had unlocked the woman's pent-up desires. She pressed even closer to him, her breasts crushing between them until Slocum felt the pounding of her pulse through the lust-hard twin points.

"This isn't the place," he said. They were alone but there wasn't anywhere to spread a blanket without lying on glass fragments and cactuses, even if they had a blanket with them.

"You're just not inventive enough, John. I'm surprised at you." Maddy worked at his trousers and unbuttoned them while he unfastened his cross-draw holster. She scooted his pants down around his ankles until he was bare-assed and shivering slightly in the wind.

"Hope I don't have to make a run for it," he said. He was almost pinned to the spot with his trousers this way.

"I kind of like it this way," she said, kneeling in front of him. He felt her hot breath across his groin and gasped when soft, wet lips closed around the tip of his hardening manhood. Her hands gripped his behind and pulled him closer to her face.

Just when Slocum thought he couldn't control himself a second longer, Maddy moved away. Cold wind whipped across tender flesh that had been so warmly housed just a second earlier. He thought he'd turn into an icicle.

"What's going on?" He opened his eyes and watched as she kicked out of her own tight britches. For a moment he thought she had turned to a statue chiseled from marble. The moon cast its light and turned her into something more than a lovely woman. Then the illusion shattered as Maddy moved, pressing close to Slocum again and rubbing up and down like a friendly cat.

"You didn't think you were going to have all the pleasure, did you?"

"I was getting around to thinking that," Slocum admitted. Then he was kissing the woman hard, his lips moving from hers to her throat and lower. The front of her vest had come open. Slocum's mouth found the tight, hard points of her breasts and sucked on them, using his tongue and teeth and lips until Maddy moaned constantly.

"Yes, John, yes, yes. Don't stop. Keep going."

The pressure of her hands on his shoulders pushed him into a squat. This was what the woman sought because she stepped up and planted her feet outside his. Then she lowered her body until she squatted above him, her nether lips brushing lightly over the tip of his erection.

"Can we—?"

"Do it," she ordered. "I need it." Maddy sank down even farther, and Slocum's once cold organ was again plunged into wet warmth. Surrounding him completely, Maddy began grinding her hips. From his squatting position, Slocum couldn't move much, but he didn't have to. Maddy was doing just fine giving them both all the delight they could handle.

Slocum kept his face low, licking and sucking at her nipples as they bobbed around. His arms circled her body and came to rest on the firm half-moons of her buttocks. He guided her in the motion that gave him the best chance of prolonging this joy for a few minutes longer.

"You're so big inside me, John. I've missed that. I've missed the feelings for so long, ever since Joseph died."

He wished she hadn't mentioned her dead husband. Slocum wasn't going to stop, but it took some of the delight from their lovemaking. If it detracted from his enjoyment, it seemed to add to the woman's. She moved faster, her body straining, turning, twisting, demanding ever more.

Whatever she sought, she got it. Maddy shivered like a leaf in a high wind and clung fiercely to Slocum as she rode out her ecstasy. He let her move for a few more seconds, then straightened his legs and stood. She hung on him like a dead weight, wiggling a little to let him know she was still enjoying it, and got her legs locked around his waist. Standing, he rocked her back and forth until he felt the hot tides rising within his loins. She shuddered and gasped loudly again as the white-hot rush geysered forth into her yearning interior. Then the woman sighed and relaxed, her legs dropping away from his body and her feet once more finding the ground.

"That was spectacular," she said, leaning against him. But Slocum wondered. He had enjoyed it, but the thought that he was only a stand-in for her dead husband kept coming back to haunt him.

17

"The engineer has agreed to collect the rest of his money after your last Salt Lake City performance," Slocum told Baron Fenstermacher. "I don't reckon there's much chance of getting back the money you paid the other engineer, though it wasn't owed him. He's obviously in cahoots with Wilkins, but there's no way to prove it, and you didn't get a receipt from him, not that it would do much good."

"We rode his train, we paid, and that is fair. But we did not use the other train. This is so confused, and people are losing money because of me. I am sorry for this. I wish Kincaid had not turned traitor and sold us out as he did. In America there are so many strange things." The baron paced nervously, making Slocum want to grab his lariat and hogtie the man before he drove him crazy. "I enjoy this country so much for its wildness and beauty, but it is so different from my home on the Continent."

"Do you know Adam Bogardus?" Slocum asked suddenly. The baron's bushy eyebrows rose and his mustache twitched. He began fiddling with the tips, making Slocum even more uneasy.

"I know him," the baron said cautiously. "Why do you ask this of me?"

"Wilkins isn't smart enough to think up all the tricks he's been pulling. Fact is, the man's not bright enough to come in from out of the rain without someone telling him he's getting wet. I didn't know Dellman, but he didn't look to be much better."

"Dellman? Pah, he was nothing. He was dimwitted. He was of no real importance or skill." The baron tapped the side of his head, although Slocum knew Dellman wasn't that stupid. Fear had gotten him killed, not stupidity.

"Tell me about it. About you and Bogardus."

"There is nothing to tell," the baron said. "The captain offered to buy the circus for very little before we started this tour. I laughed at him. The circus has been in my family for three generations. My son will be ringmaster, when I have a son." The baron let out a deep sigh of resignation. "Four daughters I have, all back in Chicago with their mama. Daily I wait for news of a son, but no. My Maria is weeks overdue." He paced even more furiously as he thought of his distant family. Slocum closed his eyes to keep from watching.

"So Bogardus wants your circus? Was the offer a good one?"

"It was nothing. The man is crazy if he thinks a Fenstermacher sells out so cheaply. We may not make a lot of money, but we do fine. Salt Lake City will prove that."

"That's the last stop you have in common with the Sells Brothers Circus?"

"I believe this is so. I have asked around. They head due west for the coast. We go north. There is not so many people, but they are appreciative and will see what Baron Fenstermacher's Fabulous Continental Circus offers them in entertainment!"

Slocum spent a few more minutes with the baron, then excused himself. He was getting more publicity than fact from the excited man. The worst would be over for the baron come Salt Lake City and the direct competition from the other circus. Slocum snorted in disgust. Kincaid had been paid handsomely to ruin the circus, but was it Wilkins or Bogardus who had done the bribery? And did it even matter? The other circus' superior collection of exotic animals almost guaranteed better attendance at their shows.

Baron Fenstermacher tottered on the brink of disaster at every venue.

When it came, maybe at Salt Lake City, Adam Bogardus would swoop down like some carrion bird and make another offer. At least, that was the way Slocum saw it.

Other thoughts crept up on him but were chased away when Madeleine interrupted him.

"John? There's something I wanted to say, but—" She chewed on her lower lip and looked flustered.

"Just go on and spit it out. That's usually the best way of getting something hard said." He had a notion what she was going to say, and he wasn't sure if it wasn't for the best. He enjoyed her company, but he felt he competed for her affections with a ghost. That was a contest he could never win.

She hesitated long enough to be interrupted by the baron calling out to them. He waved frantically, and Slocum knew that the Siren's call of her employer would erase whatever she had meant to say. And it did. Maddy turned and hurried off, muttering to herself.

He watched her trim figure and felt as if a door had closed. Whatever there was between them was gone. He had been a substitute for her lost husband and nothing more. Maybe. Slocum followed at a more leisurely pace, thinking hard. It wasn't easy figuring Madeleine Scowcroft out, and he had to decide if she was worth staying with the baron's circus any longer.

"Come, come, listen closely," Baron Fenstermacher called. "We are in a big city at last, and we will give the performance of our lives!" He strutted around, a different figure than the dejected soul who had sat in the mud and decried his fate. Success did strange things to people. The baron thrived on it, Slocum decided. And that made him worry even more. Dealing with success was a sometime thing. Baron Fenstermacher didn't handle failure well.

"We must get the crowds. To do this I am proposing a public spectacle."

Slocum made no comment at this. The circus performers were dressed in their costumes. Simply walking the streets of Salt Lake City would be a spectacle the staid residents would seldom have seen. With a few of the animals brought along, the audience would come flocking.

"I'm not sure I'm up for this, John," Maddy whispered.

"What's that?" Slocum's thoughts had been drifting. The baron had yet to come to the point. Turning his attention back to the small, mustached man, he heard nothing to indicate what the plan to draw the big crowds was going to be.

"He wants us to challenge the Bogardus Shooting Team again. I know it. I've heard this kind of pitch before. He makes a big deal out of something, builds up how courageous everyone is, then whoever he's talking about is stuck doing it."

"Or they have to back down in front of the rest of the circus," Slocum finished. He didn't cotton much to this kind of maneuvering to make people go against their wishes.

"That's it," she said with a deep sigh of resignation. Madeleine Scowcroft might blackmail like this but Slocum didn't. He would call the baron's bluff, if it came to that. His shoulder still ached from the last shoot-out, and he was thinking of getting on his horse and just riding off. He had enough money in his pocket to tide him over for several months. She turned to him and stared into his green eyes and saw what he was planning.

"John," she said in a voice that broke with strain. "Please. For me. There's no one else who can shoot with them. You're good, very good."

Baron Fenstermacher cried out, "I propose to put our great sharpshooters against theirs with a *ten-thousand-dollar* wager!"

This brought Slocum around, eyes wide with astonishment.

"I can't do that," he said. "I might beat Wilkins fair and square, but Billy is damned good."

"I know," she said. "The boy respects you. That might give us an edge. Together we can win, John. Please."

"Don't let him put you under this kind of—" Slocum bit off his words when a loud cheer went up in the assembled circus workers. Several came over and clapped Slocum on the back, giving their congratulations and best wishes. He started to tell the baron to call it off when a cold voice boomed out.

"We accept!"

All eyes turned to the tall, stout man decked out in a cavalry officer's full dress uniform. From the gold, Slocum saw this was a captain. He was slower to understand.

"Bogardus!" hissed Maddy.

"We accept under any conditions. The Bogardus Shooting Team is once more at full strength since I arrived last night from St. Louis."

"I'll have the flyers distributed right away," Fenstermacher shouted, gesturing grandly. "The shoot-out can commence this afternoon at one o'clock."

"Wait," Slocum protested. "Who's going to shoot?"

"Billy is under the weather with the ague," Bogardus said. "Therefore, Clay Wilkins and I will represent the Sells Brothers Circus. Who will defend the baron's honor?" The way he said it carried a sneer that put Slocum's teeth on edge.

"I will," Maddy spoke up. She moved a little closer to Slocum and gripped his arm.

"There have to be local representatives checking the targets and doing the throwing." Slocum didn't want any part of this but had to be sure Maddy wasn't cheated again. She gripped harder on his arm, but he refused to be herded into this corral.

To hell with the baron and his coercion, and even to hell with Maddy for trying to get him to go along with the shoot-out for such an outrageous amount of money. The only outcome for Slocum would be loss. If they failed to outshoot Bogardus, the baron lost—and it would be on Slocum's head. And if they won, Slocum wasn't likely to see any part of that prodigious wager. He'd be lucky to get Baron Fenstermacher's sincere thanks for being such a good marksman.

"Done," Bogardus said, still sneering. He watched Slocum like a vulture waiting for its dinner to die.

Slocum returned the gaze evenly, wondering what it was that bothered him so about the man. Wearing a Union cavalry officer's uniform was unusual, but something more than that niggled at the back of Slocum's mind. Some small item refused to fall into place and that bothered Slocum.

"Do you have the time?" Bogardus asked, eyes boring into Slocum's.

Slocum went cold inside.

"It's time to shatter your reputation," he said. "I'll be shooting for Baron Fenstermacher's Fabulous Continental Circus."

A cheer went up, and Maddy let out a breath she'd been holding for too long. She leaned against him for a moment and whispered a soft thank you, then hurried off to prepare. Slocum continued to stare at Adam Bogardus. The man executed a mocking salute, did a military about-face and marched off, head high and whistling *Garry Owen,* an old Irish drinking song that had been Custer's favorite.

Slocum was going to see that Bogardus ended up the same way.

"We don't have near enough ammunition," Maddy fretted. She polished the stock of her rifle, as if this would improve her aim.

"We're going to need more than a single rifle apiece," Slocum said. "My rifle barrel got so hot during the last shoot-out that I think it's out of alignment."

"I've got several spares," Maddy said, still distracted. "How could the baron make such a large bet? And why did Bogardus have to be standing there when he vented off his steam?"

"This will be for the best," Slocum said. "We can win, if it's a fair match. I want to make sure the local people chosen to watch over the match are honest and not ringers like that fake preacher man."

"The baron will see to that. I'm worried, John. I can beat Bogardus. I *know* I can, but what if I don't?"

She looked stricken. To her it was a matter of reputation. For Slocum this match had turned into something more.

"So we lose," he said.

"But the baron will lose the circus. That has to be the only result. He doesn't have ten thousand dollars. Adam Bogardus is a rich man, the baron isn't."

"Never wager money you can't afford to lose. That's the rule I follow when I'm dealing cards." Slocum examined the rifle rack holding Maddy's spare rifles. He took out three and worked their levers, noting how carefully they had been maintained. He appreciated her gunsmithing, but he wanted to sight them in for himself. He undoubtedly favored a different sight picture when shooting.

"We can go out back. The town marshal said we could practice till the match." She looked even more nervous. "What time is it?"

"We have time," Slocum said, remembering Bogardus's question and the leer behind it.

They took the rifles and set up targets at twenty yards, about the distance Slocum figured they would be shooting. He got a sand bag and hunkered down, the rifle carefully resting in a hollow. He fired several times but wasn't satisfied. The targets broke, but he knew none were dead center, as he preferred.

"I've got tools, John." Maddy passed over a small oilskin pouch. He opened it and saw the assortment of wrenches needed to properly sight in a rifle.

"I'm going to put a newspaper around the target to be sure where the slug is hitting." He went and nailed up a sheet and placed the target squarely in the middle. He could tell in an instant where the rifle was firing and correct it.

"Think you can hit it now, Slocum?"

Slocum turned and saw Clay Wilkins standing on a boardwalk, arms crossed, looking relaxed.

"Reckon I need some incentive," Slocum said, turning toward Wilkins and cocking the rifle. He didn't lift it too far when the man let out a screech of fear.

"Don't shoot, damn your eyes! I'm not armed!"

"Get out of here, Wilkins. We're getting ready."

Wilkins regained some small portion of courage, though he licked his lips nervously. Slocum got scant satisfaction from it. He ought to have put the bullet through Wilkins's worthless carcass and to hell with the match.

But there was Bogardus and what he had insinuated about Slocum's watch. Slocum had to know for sure.

"You heard the lady. Hightail it or maybe I'll just put a bullet through your knee. Any druthers which one?" Slocum shifted the rifle from his right to his left hand. "This might make it more sporting, me shooting left-handed."

"You're going to lose the circus for the old man," Wilkins called out. "You're the ones who are going to be out of jobs by this afternoon. Wait and see!" He swallowed hard, eyed Slocum to be sure he wasn't going to shoot him in the back, then turned and almost fled in fear.

"We did some good," Slocum said, returning to the sand bag and settling the rifle in firmly.

"What's that?"

"We brought a tad of fear to the surface. Inside he must be seething now. Any edge we can get helps us out." Slocum fired four times, studied the shot pattern and began working on the sights to get them into perfect alignment.

"Yes," Maddy said softly. "Any edge, any edge. We're going to need it against Bogardus."

The match began one hour later.

18

"What a most excellent crowd," Baron Fenstermacher chortled. He rubbed his hands together and looked as if he didn't have a care in the world. Slocum knew the man was risking the existence of his circus. Bogardus would take the title, lock, stock, and barrel, and leave the baron with nothing more than the flashy ringmaster's costume he wore.

And given half a chance, Bogardus would take even that. Slocum didn't kid himself about the sharpshooter's motives or generosity. He had seen the way the captain stared at Maddy. Slocum wasn't sure if getting her under contract wasn't Bogardus's sole purpose in wanting the circus. She was not only a good sharpshooter, she was a beautiful woman.

"There must be five hundred people here," muttered Maddy, obviously nervous about the match. They had arranged with the local marshal to hold the shoot-out on the outskirts of Salt Lake City. It had taken almost twenty minutes to assemble their gear, find enough ammunition for a two-thousand-shot match, and get out to the muddy flats. Not five miles off stretched the Great Salt Lake.

"More," Slocum said. He didn't cotton much to big crowds of people, but that wasn't what put him on edge. Bogardus wouldn't simply let himself be outshot, even if Maddy or Slocum could do it. The tricks Wilkins had pulled were nothing compared to those Bogardus might have up his sleeve.

Slocum smiled crookedly. Or maybe not. Overweening pride might drive Bogardus. He might not think it was possible for a woman and a drifter to outgun him, no matter what Clay Wilkins or Billy might have told him.

Slocum laid the rifles on the small table and looked toward the lake. A dozen stout men had been chosen to toss the targets. Another dozen had been given a dollar each to inspect the feather-filled glass spheres for cracks or other defects. If any were found, it was to be discarded. On this score Slocum had no problem.

When Wilkins lugged up the Bogardus Shooting Team's boxes of ammo, he saw Wilkins's sly look. The man had doctored the ammunition and didn't think Slocum knew. Slocum went about his business unconcernedly, then laid his rifle on the table and wandered over to a small knot of spectators from the city.

"This must be bringing good business to you," Slocum said after a few pleasantries.

"How's that?" asked a man who had the look of a shopkeeper about him.

"We had to buy a half-dozen boxes of ammo. Reckon Bogardus had to do the same."

The man scratched his bald pate and shook his head, as if worrying over the idea. "Can't say they bought any from me, but there's a dozen other places in Salt Lake City that might have sold 'em the cartridges."

"That brand?" Slocum said, pointing. "That's the same as you sold us."

"Now that's peculiar. I'm the only supply for it along the rail line this side of Denver. Must have brought it with 'em from out of town. You folks travelin' around have it made, always seein' new places. This is God's chosen city, it is, but sometimes I get the wanderlust." He gazed longingly toward the west and the distant purple-hazed mountains. Slocum knew the feeling and was getting itchy feet, too.

"That's a good brand of ammunition," observed Slocum.

"It is that. Never heard of any misfires."

"All the cartridges are essentially identical," Slocum pressed.

"Yes," the shopkeeper said, staring at him strangely. Slocum said nothing more and returned to the table. He had learned a bit from Baron Fenstermacher when it came to enlisting people's aid without them intending it.

"Are you ready to shoot?" asked Maddy. "I'm so nervous my hands are shaking. I've never gone up against a legend before."

Slocum snorted. Some legend, if his suspicions were right. He didn't burden Maddy with them at the moment.

"I can shoot with Bogardus and you can take Wilkins," he said. They had agreed to fire in pairs, one from each team, until none missed a target. The other two would take up the pace and fire until one of them missed. With a thousand targets for each to be tossed, it would be a long afternoon— and possibly longer. Slocum had heard the baron arguing with the marshal about bonfires if the match lasted longer than seven hours and light was required to continue.

Slocum did some quick ciphering in his head and decided they'd have to average better than one shot every thirty seconds to finish in that time. He rubbed his shoulder and worked the stiffness from it. Before nightfall, he knew he would be hurting something fierce.

"May I make a suggestion?" The voice was familiar. Slocum looked up and saw the circus vet, Dr. Poussard. The man held out a bottle of strong smelling liniment. "This works as good on men as it does on horses and elephants."

"Thanks." Slocum sprinkled some onto his right hand and rubbed it into his shoulder. Within minutes the soreness was gone. He didn't know if it removed it for all time or just gave him a few minutes before coming back. He had enough in the bottle to last the afternoon.

"You might want a swig of this, too." The vet held out a silver flask.

"Not right now. Maybe later," Slocum said, wanting to keep a clear head and sharp eye. Fatigue would set in before long. Then it would serve to cut through the pall of exhaustion that would rob him of pinpoint accuracy.

"Be careful about the water bucket," Poussard warned. "Heard stories of them putting alum in it to make their opponents so thirsty they give up or pass out." He pointed to a small keg brimming with water. The sight of it made Slocum's dry mouth yearn for cool liquid.

"Have the baron bring us some for our own use," Slocum said, worried that Maddy hadn't tended to this already. She was too concerned over Bogardus's reputation to think clearly. The vet nodded and hurried off.

"Ladies and gentlemen of the fine, gracious city of Salt Lake, we will see a performance unheralded in the annals of sharpshooting," bellowed the baron. "Today Miss Madeleine Scowcroft and Mr. John Slocum will each attempt to break one thousand targets *each*!"

"And," cut in Adam Bogardus, "the Bogardus Shooting Team will *succeed* in this feat! Let the match begin!"

Slocum and Wilkins were to start. Slocum walked to the mark drawn in the muddy ground where he was to shoot. He hesitated, then went to the table holding both teams' ammo. He took a box and dumped it out on the table—then grabbed Wilkins' and dumped it onto the table, the cartridges rolling together.

"What are you doing?" Wilkins grabbed Slocum's wrist and kept him from mixing up the ammunition more than he had.

"Nothing. Just thought it would be easier for us to pick up the rounds this way."

"This is special ammo we use," Wilkins protested. "We don't want you using it."

"It doesn't matter, since we're both using the same store-bought rounds," Slocum said. "Isn't that so?" he asked of the shopkeeper. "Isn't this brand noted for its reliability?"

"Surely is. Don't see that one slug is going to fly any different if it came from your box or his." The store keeper looked around, wondering if he ought to put in a plug for his emporium while he was the center of attention.

"So it really doesn't matter whose ammunition is used, since it's all the same." Slocum bore down on the last words, daring Wilkins to make an issue of it.

"That's all right, Wilkins. Let's get on with it," Bogardus said. From the sour look he gave Slocum, it had been his idea to add the birdshot behind the .44 slug in each round. This confirmed what Slocum had thought. Wilkins wasn't bright enough to think up such deviltry on his own; it had all been Adam Bogardus's doing.

Slocum loaded his rifle, not knowing if he used the doctored rounds or his own. It didn't matter. He wasn't going to miss.

The first target flew up, shining in the early afternoon sunlight. Slocum followed its trajectory smoothly, swung through its arc and fired. Feathers cascaded down on a gentle wind and a cheer went up from the crowd.

The great Salt Lake City shootout had begun.

Wilkins was the first to miss a glass sphere after eighty-eight hits. Slocum gratefully went to sit down, examine the second rifle he was going to use and to rub some of Poussard's liniment into his shoulder. Inactivity would make it start to seize up.

Maddy passed within a few feet. He saw she was still nervous. "Bust 'em all," he said softly. "You can do it."

She jumped, startled by his words. Then he watched as she settled down. Performing innumerable times had given her a stage presence that helped her now.

Bogardus condescendingly let her shoot first. A million glass shards were caught on the wind and sparked like a new sun in the air.

"Your turn, Captain," she said.

Slocum had to shoot again when Maddy missed after one hundred-eight targets.

All afternoon they shot, running through rifles that got so hot from the constant firing that the barrels began to sag. More than three score men took turns examining and throwing the feather-filled targets, some lasting only a few dozen tosses before giving out and letting another take his place. And through it all the four shooters kept up a fierce pace, enduring sun and fatigue to make one incredible shot after another. By the time the sun was sinking low in the west, the baron came over with the tally.

Slocum sat and stared, feeling as if someone had somehow separated body from soul. Never during the long watches during the war had he felt this beaten and weary. The hammering of the rifle's recoil against his shoulder had caused huge yellow and black bruises to form. The smallest movement turned to stark pain, and this was after he used the horse liniment.

"You've each shot at over nine hundred targets," the baron said, bubbling with excitement. "And you're one target ahead!"

"Just one?" Slocum said. "How many have I missed?"

"None!"

Slocum blinked. He didn't remember missing any, but he wasn't sure. That was a sure sign he was approaching collapse.

"Maddy's missed only three."

"I know Wilkins has missed several."

"Four," the baron said. "Wilkins has missed more than either of you."

Even Slocum's fatigue-besotted brain worked out the real number, the one that counted. Adam Bogardus hadn't missed a single target after shooting for almost six hours. He had matched Slocum's expertise with the rifle—and he looked as if he had just awakened from a good night's sleep. Bogardus walked around the perimeter of the crowd, shaking hands, making small jokes, urging the people to see the evening performance of the Sells Brothers Circus.

"We are going to win. The ten thousand dollars will be ours!" The baron ignored the weariness seizing Slocum's arms. He could barely lift the rifle back to his throbbing shoulder.

"You are up," called the mayor of the city. He had come to the front of the crowd an hour ago, waiting to be on hand for the finale. Slocum heaved to his feet and tried to find the calm needed to shoot accurately.

The twilight turned to darkness and still they shot on, the pace slowing as more and more misses were scored. The last hundred targets proved more difficult than the first nine hundred. Slocum missed three targets and retired with a score of 997 out of 1000, eight targets ahead of Wilkins's respectable 989 of 1000.

"We have done it, we have done it," chuckled the baron.

"Maddy's not finished," Slocum pointed out. "How many has Bogardus missed so far?"

"One," came the answer.

Slocum slumped. Bogardus had bettered him by two, but this was the captain's game. It was up to Maddy to wind the day for the baron.

"What is her score?" Slocum didn't know if he wanted the answer, but he had to ask. A boy ran and asked, returning in a few minutes with the answer.

"She's missed seven, Bogardus only one."

A gasp went up from the crowd. Maddy had missed another. And Bogardus missed the next. They settled into the home stretch, but Maddy missed one more.

"The tally, boy, get me the tally!" shouted Baron Fenstermacher. "I must know."

Slocum closed his eyes and came to the answer as the mayor announced the results.

"The Bogardus Shooting Team has a combined total of 1987—and the sharpshooters from Baron Fenstermacher's Fabulous Continental Circus have broken 1988! The baron's team wins!"

A roar went up that deafened Slocum. He knew most of the people cheering were the baron's performers and employees. They had just retained their jobs—and their boss.

Maddy came over and almost collapsed into Slocum's arms. She was sobbing. "I missed nine targets," she gasped out. "I missed nine! I almost lost the match for us."

Before Slocum could comfort her, Bogardus jumped onto the table and fired his rifle to get everyone's attention. When he had it, he boomed out, "They have won fairly, but I hasten to point out that I, Captain Adam Bogardus, scored an almost perfect round, missing only two. I personally retain the title of World's Greatest Sharpshooter!"

Slocum wondered how the score would have differed if they had used only single-slug ammunition. Some of his shots had seemed a tad off center but the spheres had broken, possibly a result of using the Bogardus-loaded birdshot rounds. But if he'd achieved a high score, Bogardus and Wilkins had the same chance.

"The wager was ten thousand dollars, to be donated to the great city of Salt Lake!"

"Wait, no, that's my money," protested the baron, but the cheer from the townspeople drowned out his protests.

"Here is your money!"

Bogardus signaled to three circus roustabouts who had come from town as the last shots in the match were being fired. A huge glass sphere arched over the crowd. He spun and fired, shattering the glass. Greenbacks rained down on the crowd. A second and a third were similarly broken, sending the usually sedate people into a frenzy of grabbing for the fluttering bills.

Slocum watched grimly. There was no way to tell if the three targets had been filled with ten thousand dollars or some lesser sum. Knowing Bogardus, it was probably only a few hundred, but no one in the town would ever admit that. They had a story to tell their children and grandchildren yet unborn about the day it had rained money from the sky.

The shooting match was ended, but Slocum still had unfinished business to settle with Clay Wilkins and Adam Bogardus.

19

"The money," moaned Baron Fenstermacher. "We lost the money. I can't believe it. The money!" He walked, head hanging down like a whipped dog. Slocum had no time for him. He was aching and exhausted from the afternoon of shooting.

He stopped when he saw Maddy just standing and staring numbly across the Great Salt Lake, arms hanging limp at her sides. Tears welled in her eyes but hadn't yet begun running down her dusty cheeks. He went to her, knowing what would happen. She turned and just stared, the coal dark eyes devoid of expression.

"He cheated us, John. We beat him, and he still won."

"No, we won. He had to pay, though it wasn't quite the way the baron had intended. I have to give Bogardus this much. He's one hell of a showman."

"I had the chance to beat him and I failed. I missed more than he did. I could have won, and I didn't. I'm a loser."

"This isn't an easy job, Maddy," said Slocum. He winced as he moved. The veterinarian's liniment had helped; Slocum didn't want to think what agony he would be enduring now if he hadn't used it so liberally on his shoulder all day. "Bogardus has been doing this for a lot longer than you have."

"It doesn't matter."

"It does," he assured her. "And you beat Wilkins by two targets. I'd say we all shot damned good today."

"I suppose you're right," she said, wiping away the tears. "That doesn't make it any easier to swallow that he beat me by seven targets. Seven! I'm better than that."

"You were going up against two opponents today," Slocum told her. "You were firing against Bogardus and also against his reputation. You can beat the man. You'll never win against a myth."

"I beat myself? Is that what you're saying?"

He didn't answer because there was no need. She knew what had gone wrong. He could tell her a thousand times, and she'd never listen. Only when Maddy felt it in her heart and got a tad of confidence in her abilities would it matter.

"I've got business to tend to in town." He put his hand on her shoulder and squeezed reassuringly, then went to fetch his horse.

"John, you're leaving, aren't you? You won't be around after the performance tonight."

"It seems best for both of us."

"I need you, John. I love you."

"No, you don't. I remind you of Joseph. I can't beat a memory any more than you can whip a myth."

"Please, just for tonight."

"I've got business to tend to, then we'll see." He saw her wipe at more tears and chew on her lower lip. What he did was for the best—and he might not be around for the evening show, even if he wanted to be. He had a score to settle with Clay Wilkins.

And Adam Bogardus.

The entire Bogardus Shooting Team had packed up their wagon and rolled back into Salt Lake City. Slocum went to their encampment and asked for them. The roustabouts were setting up for the Sells Brothers's evening exhibition and hadn't seen any of the sharpshooters, but all had heard of the match's outcome.

That told Slocum where to find both Wilkins and Bogardus. He rode slowly through the streets of the clean, peaceful town looking to create some mayhem. It took more than an hour for him to find the small building at the outskirts of town where liquor was served. He dismounted and tied his horse to a hitching post. Shrugging, he got his left shoulder moving easy, then took the leather thong off the hammer of his Colt. It was time to settle scores.

He went into the clandestine saloon and looked around. This was a world away from most dance halls he frequented. No whores were in sight, and the few men drinking did so almost sedately. There was some raucous laughter but it died quickly. Slocum didn't know if it was just that way in a saloon virtually forbidden in Salt Lake City or if it was because they had seen him—and knew he was looking for serious trouble.

"What'll it be?" asked the barkeep. Slocum noticed that the man kept his hands under the bar, probably resting on the triggers of a double-barreled shotgun.

"Clay Wilkins. You seen him? Or Bogardus?"

"The galoots from the circus? They was here but left almost an hour ago."

The way the bartender's eyes darted away when he spoke told Slocum he was lying. He wanted to avoid trouble. Slocum didn't doubt for an instant this gin mill was barely tolerated and any real fuss here would bring down the wrath of the church.

Slocum nodded and walked slowly to the rear of the saloon. A side door stood open a few inches. Not five feet away a green-felt-topped table still held two shot glasses and a quarter-bottle of whiskey. Slocum popped the cork out of the bottle and took a short pull. It went down his gullet warm and smooth and burned as it puddled in his belly. No man walked away from a bottle of good whiskey. He glanced over his shoulder and saw the barkeep's expression. He didn't need to be told the men he sought had slipped out seconds before he entered.

Putting the bottle back on the table, Slocum went to the door and pushed it open with his toe, staying well back. No bullets ripped through the open space. Slocum whirled through the door, not wanting to outline himself against the light more than necessary to get outside.

"I shoulda killed you a long time ago, Slocum," came a quavering voice.

"You ever kill a man you were looking in the eye, Wilkins?" Slocum kept walking until he found the shadow hiding Wilkins. "Or do you only bushwhack them?"

"I'm the best damned gun-handler in the West." The way Wilkins spoke, he'd had too much to drink. Slocum didn't care. If a man carried a six-shooter, he had to be completely responsible for his own actions.

"You been trying everything under the sun to stop me," Slocum said. "You rigged a fight, you framed me for robbery and murder, you—"

"You're a dead man, Slocum. Draw!"

Even as Wilkins cried out his challenge, Slocum was going for his pistol. His right hand twitched slightly; the tension of firing all afternoon had taken its toll on more than his shoulder. But the Colt Navy came easily from its holster. The familiar smoothness of aiming and firing was second nature to Slocum. He didn't have to check to see if his bullet had hit where he aimed.

Clay Wilkins never uttered a sound. He simply sank to his knees, his pistol half out of its holster. Tottering for another second, he tried to finish the draw and couldn't. He fell face down in the dirt, Slocum's single bullet having ripped out his heart.

"You're about the fastest man I ever saw," came a cold voice from behind. "If you try turning, I'll blow your head off. And don't doubt that I am capable. I hit all but two of a thousand flying targets today. You don't pose half the problem of any of those."

"Is backshooting the way the famous Captain Bogardus works?"

"Can't say I have anything against it." Bogardus laughed harshly. "Go on, Slocum. Move. Move and I'll plug you through the head, as I did Dellman."

"So it was you who framed me," Slocum said. His six-shooter hung uselessly in his hand. He needed to turn and fire, but he felt the sights of Bogardus's rifle centered on his back. He'd never be able to do what needed doing in time.

"Of course it was. Wilkins was a fool. He had some talent, but thinking wasn't included. Billy makes a much better draw for the crowd than Wilkins ever did. He's a better shot, and he can be trained."

"Why'd you kill Dellman?"

"He knew I'd returned early from St. Louis and set you up for the bank job. I planned it all."

"And you killed Sheriff Mallory's deputy?"

"I might have. I didn't ask to see his badge. It was a long way off, getting dark, and I was just downright proud to hit my target on the first shot."

"What are you going to do, Bogardus?"

"I could just walk away. You killed Wilkins. That ought to get the Salt Lake marshal riled a mite. They don't like outsiders coming to their fine town and shooting it up, even when the victim is another drifter."

"You could do that, but you're not."

"Why not?" taunted Bogardus.

"Because I'll find you and cut you down wherever you run."

"That's right, Slocum. I'm not going to let the law handle this for the very reason you said. Since you showed up, everything's gone wrong. You exposed Kincaid and ruined my chance for buying the baron's circus. I really do want to get away from the Sells Brothers Circus and run my own. Mine can be bigger and better than any other in the West, thanks to my sharpshooting skill. And Maddy would make quite an addition to the Bogardus Shooting Team." The way he said it, Bogardus intended more for Madeleine Scowcroft than being an employee.

"So I'm the cause of all your trouble?" Slocum took a deep breath. He had to act and fast.

"Oh, no, but you have fouled my plans for the last time."

The hammer on the Winchester cocked.

Slocum feinted to the right and whirled left, his six-shooter coming around. He landed hard on the ground, his gun arm under him and Colt aimed toward where he thought Bogardus stood.

A rifle blazed but the bullet missed Slocum by a country mile. He struggled to get his gun on target, his shoulder paining him something fierce.

"Whoa, hold your horses, Slocum. It's all under control."

A man stood over a dark heap. Light from inside the saloon glinted off a sheriff's badge.

Slocum carefully rose, his six-shooter staying on the standing man. He walked toward the shadowy figure until light showed him that he faced Sheriff Mallory.

"Came by to pull your nuts out of the fire at just the right time, didn't I?" Sheriff Mallory stared down at Bogardus, who moaned and stirred. Mallory stretched and obviously experienced a pang of pain. "Still not back to my usual nasty self," he said. Mallory kicked Bogardus hard.

"He's the one who bushwhacked you."

"I heard. And he killed Little Al, too. Heard the other confessions. Reckon I got myself a real killer here, not to mention bank robber and a passel of other things." Mallory grabbed Bogardus by the collar and heaved him to his feet.

"Aren't you a ways from your jurisdiction?"

"That's a fact, but I'll track a man to the ends of the earth if I have to. Lucas can handle things back home for a spell. Leastwise I figure that's true. Didn't take me long to figure out who the culprit might be. Took me a sight longer to heal up enough to do something about it."

Slocum slid his Colt Navy back into its holster when he saw a half-dozen men with sawed-off shotguns hurrying down the street.

"The local law is coming to see what the ruckus is," Slocum said.

"Damnation. I hoped to get him out of here without arguing with them. Why don't you just fade into the night, Slocum? I can handle this by myself."

Slocum hesitated, then looked from Mallory to the approaching marshal and the deputies with him. He nodded to Mallory, then stepped back and became one with the shadows. He heard the dispute begin over what crime had been committed, who had the right to arrest the prisoner, and then Bogardus found his voice and loudly demanded to be released.

Slocum had no concern that Sheriff Mallory would let the sharpshooter off scot-free. It was no more in his character than it was in Slocum's.

He walked slowly around the saloon, found his sorrel, and mounted. From the other end of town came the music and sounds of Baron Fenstermacher's Fabulous Continental Circus. He could ride that way and see if he'd got things wrong with Maddy. He might have misunderstood her, and she might not be looking for another Joseph. Slocum thought for a moment, then turned his horse's face for the high country and put his spurs to the sorrel's flanks.

It was time to move on.

November 24, 1863—Just east of Chattanooga, Tennessee

The chestnut stallion's head snapped up very suddenly. Its nostrils quivered, then flared, testing the wind, tasting the approach of unseen danger. Old Justin Ballou's watchful eye caught the stallion's motion and he also froze, senses focused. For several long moments, man and stallion remained motionless, and then Justin Ballou opened the gate to the paddock and limped toward the tall Thoroughbred. He reached up and his huge, blue-veined hand stroked the stallion's muzzle. "What is it, High Man?" he asked softly. "What now, my friend?"

In answer, the chestnut dipped its head several times and stamped its feet with increasing nervousness. Justin began to speak soothingly to the stallion, his deep, resonant voice flowing like a mystical incantation. Almost at once, the stallion grew calm. After a few minutes, Justin said, as if to an old and very dear friend, "Is it one of General Grant's Union patrols this time, High Man? Have they come to take what little I have left? If so, I will gladly fight them to the death."

The stallion shook its head, rolled its eyes, and snorted as if it could smell Yankee blood. Justin's thick fingers scratched a special place behind the stallion's ear. The chestnut lowered its head to nuzzle the man's chest.

"Don't worry. It's probably another Confederate patrol," Justin said thoughtfully. "But what can they want this time? I have already given them three fine sons and most of your offspring. There is so little left to give—but they know that! Surely they can see my empty stalls and paddocks."

Justin turned toward the road leading past his neat, whitewashed fences that sectioned and cross-sectioned his famous Tennessee horse ranch, known throughout the South as Wildwood Farm. The paddocks were empty and silent. This cold autumn day, there were proud mares with their colts, and prancing fillies blessed the old man's vision or gave him the joy he'd known for so many years. It was the war—this damned killing Civil War. "No more!" Justin cried. "You'll have no more of my fine horses or sons!"

The stallion spun and galloped away. High Man was seventeen years old, long past his prime, but he and a few other Ballou-bred stallions still sired the fastest and handsomest horses in the South. Just watching the chestnut run made Justin feel a little better. High Man was a living testimony to the extraordinarily fine care he'd received all these years at Wildwood Farms. No one would believe that at his ripe age he could still run and kick his heels up like a three-year-old colt.

The stallion ran with such fluid grace that he seemed to float across the earth. When the Thoroughbred reached the far end of the paddock, it skidded to a sliding stop, chest banging hard against the fence. It spun around, snorted, and shook its head for an expected shout of approval.

But not this day. Instead, Justin made himself leave the paddock, chin up, stride halting but resolute. He could hear thunder growing louder. Could it be the sound of cannon from as far away as the heights that General Bragg and his Rebel army now held in wait of the Union army's expected assault? No, the distance was too great even to carry the roar of heavy artillery. That told Justin that his initial hunch was correct and the sound growing in his ears had to be racing hoofbeats.

But were they enemy or friend? Blue coat or gray? Justin planted his big work boots solidly in the dust of the country road, either way, he would meet them.

"Father!"

He recognized his fourteen-year-old daughter's voice and ignored it, wanting Dixie to stay inside their mansion. Justin drew a pepperbox pistol from his waistband. If this actually was a dreaded Union cavalry patrol, then someone was going to die this afternoon. A man could only be pushed so far and then he had to fight.

"Father!" Dixie's voice was louder now, more strident. "Father!"

Justin reluctantly twisted about to see his daughter and her oldest brother, Houston, running toward him. Both had guns clenched in their fists.

"Who is it?" Houston gasped, reaching Justin first and trying to catch his wind.

Justin did not dignify the stupid question with an answer. In a very few minutes, they would know. "Dixie, go back to the house."

"Please, I . . . I just can't!"

"Dixie! Do as Father says," Houston stormed. "This is no time for arguing. Go to the house!"

Dixie's black eyes sparked. She stood her ground. Houston was twenty-one and a man full grown, but he was still just her big brother. "I'm staying."

Houston's face darkened with anger and his knuckles whitened as he clutched the gun in his fist. "Dammit, you heard . . ."

"Quiet, the both of you!" Justin commanded. "Here they come."

A moment later a dust-shrouded patrol lifted from the earth to come galloping up the road.

"It's *our* boys," Dixie yelped with relief. "It's a Reb patrol!"

"Yeah," Houston said, taking an involuntary step forward, "but they been shot up all to hell!"

Justin slipped his gun back into his waistband and was seized by a flash of dizziness. Dixie moved close, steadying him until the spell passed a moment later. "You all right?"

Justin nodded. He did not know what was causing the dizziness, but the spells seemed to come often these days. No doubt, it was the war. This damned war that the South was steadily losing. And the death of two of his five strapping sons and . . .

Houston had stepped out in front and now he turned to shout, "Mason is riding with them!"

Justin's legs became solid and strong again. Mason was the middle son, the short, serious one that wanted to go into medicine and who read volumes of poetry despite the teasing from his brothers.

Dixie slipped her gun into the pocket of the loose-fitting pants she insisted on wearing around the horses. She glanced up at her father and said, "Mason will be hungry and so will the others. They'll need food and bandaging."

"They'll have both," Justin declared without hesitation, "but no more of my Thoroughbreds!"

"No more," Dixie vowed. "Mason will understand."

"Yeah," Houston said, coming back to stand by his father, "but the trouble is, he isn't in charge. That's a captain he's riding alongside."

Justin was about to speak, but from the corner of his eyes, saw a movement. He twisted, hand instinctively lifting the pepperbox because these woods were crawling with both Union and Confederate deserters, men often half-crazy with fear and hunger.

"Pa, don't you dare shoot me!" Rufus "Ruff" Ballou called, trying to force a smile as he moved forward, long and loose limbed with his rifle swinging at his side.

"Ruff, what the hell you doing hiding in those trees!" Houston demanded, for he too had been startled enough to raise his gun.

If Ruff noticed the heat in his older brother's voice, he chose to ignore it.

"Hell, Houston, I was just hanging back a little to make sure these were friendly visitors."

"It's Mason," Justin said, turning back to the patrol. "And from the looks of these boys, things are going from bad to worse."

There were just six men in the patrol, two officers and four enlisted. One of the enlisted was bent over nearly double with pain, a blossom of red spreading across his left shoulder. Two others were riding double on a runty sorrel.

"That sorrel is gonna drop if it don't get feed and rest," Ruff observed, his voice hardening with disapproval.

"All of their mounts look like they've been chased to hell and back without being fed or watered," Justin stated. "We'll make sure they're watered and grained before these boys leave."

The Ballous nodded. It never occurred to any of them that a horse should ever leave their farm in worse shape then when it had arrived. The welfare of livestock just naturally came first—even over their own physical needs.

Justin stepped forward and raised his hand in greeting. Deciding that none of the horses were in desperate circumstances, he fixed his attention on Mason. He was shocked. Mason was a big man, like his father and brothers, but now he appeared withered—all ridges and angles. His cap was missing and his black hair was wild and unkept. His cheeks were hollow, and the sleeve of his right arm had been cut away, and now his arm was wrapped in a dirty bandage. The loose, sloppy way he sat his horse told Justin more eloquently than words how weak and weary Mason had become after just eight months of fighting the armies of the North.

The patrol slowed to a trot, then a walk, and Justin saw the captain turn to speak to Mason. Justin couldn't hear the words, but he could see by the senior officer's expression that the man was angry and upset. Mason rode trancelike, eyes fixed on his family, lips a thin, hard slash instead of the expected smile of greeting.

Mason drew his horse to a standstill before his father and brothers. Up close, his appearance was even more shocking.

"Mason?" Justin whispered when his son said nothing. "Mason, are you all right?"

Mason blinked. Shook himself. "Father. Houston. Ruff. Dixie. You're all looking well. How are the horses?"

"What we got left are fine," Justin said cautiously. "Only a few on the place even fit to run. Sold all the fillies and colts last fall. But you knew that."

"You did the right thing to keep Houston and Ruff out of this," Mason said.

Houston and Ruff took a sudden interest in the dirt under their feet. The two youngest Ballou brothers had desperately wanted to join the Confederate army, but Justin had demanded that they remain at Wildwood Farm, where they could help carry on the family business of raising Thoroughbreds. Only now, instead of racetracks and cheering bettors, the Ballou horses swiftly carried messages between the generals of the Confederate armies. Many times the delivery of a vital message depended on horses with pure blazing speed.

"Lieutenant," the captain said, clearing his throat loudly, "I think this chatter has gone on quite long enough. Introduce me."

Mason flushed with humiliation. "Father, allow me to introduce Captain Denton."

Justin had already sized up the captain, and what he saw did not please him. Denton was a lean, straight-backed man. He rode as if he had a rod up his ass and he looked like a mannequin glued to the saddle. He was an insult to the fine tradition of Southern cavalry officers.

"Captain," Justin said without warmth, "if you'll order your patrol to dismount, we'll take care of your wounded and these horses."

"Private Wilson can't ride any farther," Denton said. "And there isn't time for rest."

"But you *have* to," Justin argued. "These horses are—"

"Finished," Denton said. "We must have replacements, that's why we are here, Mr. Ballou."

Justin paled ever so slightly. "Hate to tell you this, Captain, but I'm afraid you're going to be disappointed. I've already given all the horses I can to the Confederacy—sons, too."

Denton wasn't listening. His eyes swept across the paddock.

"What about *that* one," he said, pointing toward High Man. "He looks to be in fine condition."

"He's past his racing prime," Houston argued. "He's our foundation sire now and is used strictly for breeding."

"Strictly for breeding?" Denton said cryptically. "Mr. Ballou, there is not a male creature on this earth who would not like to—"

"Watch your tongue, sir!" Justin stormed. "My daughter's honor will not be compromised!"

Captain Denton's eyes jerked sideways to Dixie and he blushed. Obviously, he had not realized Dixie was a girl with her baggy pants and a felt slouch hat pulled down close to her eyebrows. And a Navy Colt hanging from her fist.

"My sincere apologies." The captain dismissed her and his eyes came to rest on the barns. "You've got horses in those stalls?"

"Yes, but—"

"I'd like to see them," Denton said, spurring his own flagging mount forward.

Ruff grabbed his bit. "Hold up there, Captain, you haven't been invited."

"And since when does an officer of the Confederacy need to beg permission for horses so that *your* countrymen, as well as mine, can live according to our own laws!"

"*I'm* the law on this place," Justin thundered. "And my mares are in foal. They're not going to war, Captain. Neither they nor the last of my stallions are going to be chopped to pieces on some battlefield or have their legs ruined while trying to pull supply wagons. These are *Thoroughbred* horses, sir! Horses bred to race."

"The race," Denton said through clenched teeth, "is to see if we can bring relief to our men who are, this very moment, fighting and dying at Lookout Mountain and Missionary Ridge."

Denton's voice shook with passion. "The plundering armies of General Ulysses Grant, General George Thomas, and his Army of the Cumberland are attacking our soldiers right now, and God help me if I've ever seen such slaughter! Our boys are dying, Mr. Ballou! Dying for the right to determine the South's great destiny. We—not you and your piddling horses—are making the ultimate sacrifices! But maybe your attitude has a lot to do with why you married a Cherokee Indian woman."

Something snapped behind Justin Ballou's obsidian eyes. He saw the faces of his two oldest sons, one reported to have been blown to pieces by a Union battery in the battle of Bull Run and the other trampled to death in a bloody charge at Shiloh. Their proud mother's Cherokee blood had made them the first in battle and the first in death.

Justin lunged, liver-spotted hands reaching upward. Too late Captain Denton saw murder in the old man's eyes. He tried to rein his horse off, but Justin's fingers clamped on his coat and his belt. With a tremendous heave, Denton was torn from his saddle and hurled to the ground. Justin growled like a huge dog as his fingers crushed the breath out of Denton's life.

He would have broken the Confederate captain's neck if his sons had not broken his stranglehold. Two of the mounted soldiers reached for their pistols, but Ruff's own rifle made them freeze and then slowly raise their hands.

"Pa!" Mason shouted, pulling Justin off the nearly unconscious officer. "Pa, stop it!"

As suddenly as it had flared, Justin's anger ended, and he had to be helped to his feet. He glared down at the wheezing cavalry officer and his voice trembled when he said, "Captain Denton, I don't know how the hell you managed to get a commission in Jeff Davis's army, but I do know this; lecture me about sacrifice for the South again and I will break your fool neck! Do you hear me!"

The captain's eyes mirrored raw animal fear. "Lieutenant Ballou," he choked at Mason, "I *order* you in the name of the Army of the Confederacy to confiscate fresh horses!"

"Go to hell."

"I'll have you court-martialed and shot for insubordination!"

Houston drew his pistol and aimed it at Denton's forehead. "Maybe you'd better change your tune, Captain."

"No!"

Justin surprised them all by coming to Denton's defense. "If you shoot him—no matter how much he deserves to be shot—our family will be judged traitors."

"But . . ."

"Put the gun away," Justin ordered wearily. "I'll give him fresh horses."

"Pa!" Ruff cried. "What are you going to give to him? Our mares?"

"Yes, but not all of them. Just the youngest and the strongest. And those matched three-year-old stallions you and Houston are training."

"But, Pa," Ruff protested, "they're just green broke."

"I know, but this will season them in a hurry," Justin said levelly. "Besides, there's no choice. High Man leaves Wildwood Farm over my dead body."

"Yes, sir," Ruff said, knowing his father was not running a bluff.

Dixie turned away in anger and started toward the house. "I'll see we get food cooking for the soldiers and some fresh bandages for Private Wilson."

A moment later, Ruff stepped over beside the wounded soldier. "Here, let me give you a hand down. We'll go up to the house and take a look at that shoulder."

Wilson tried to show his appreciation as both Ruff and Houston helped him to dismount. "Much obliged," he whispered. "Sorry to be of trouble."

Mason looked to his father. "Sir, I'll take responsibility for your horses."

"How can you do that?" Houston demanded of his brother. "These three-year-old stallions and our mares will go crazy amid all that cannon and rifle fire. No one but us can control them. It would be—"

"Then you and Ruff need to come on back with us," Mason said.

"No!" Justin raged. "I paid for their replacements! I've got the papers saying that they can't be drafted or taken into the Confederate army."

"Maybe not," Mason said, "but they can volunteer to help us save lives up on the mountains where General Bragg is in danger of being overrun, and where our boys are dying for lack of medical attention."

"No!" Justin choked. "I've given too much already!"

"Pa, we won't fight. We'll just go to handle the horses." Ruff placed his hand on his father's shoulder. "No fighting," he pledged, looking past his father at the road leading toward Chattanooga and the battlefields. "I swear it."

Justin shook his head, not believing a word of it. His eyes shifted from Mason to Houston and finally settled on Ruff. "You boys are *fighters*! Oh, I expect you'll even try to do as you promised, but you won't be able to once you smell gunpowder and death. You'll fight and get yourselves killed, just like Micha and John."

Mason shook his head vigorously. "Pa, I swear that once the horses are delivered and hitched to those ambulances and supply wagons, I'll send Houston and Ruff back to you. All right?"

After a long moment, Justin finally managed to nod his head. "Come along," he said to no one in particular, "we'll get our Thoroughbreds ready."

But Captain Denton's thin lips twisted in anger. "I want a *dozen* horses! Not one less will do. And I still want that big chestnut stallion in that paddock for my personal mount."

Houston scoffed with derision, "Captain, I've seen some fools in my short lifetime, but none as big as you."

"At least," Denton choked, "my daddy didn't buy my way out of the fighting."

Houston's face twisted with fury and his hand went for the Army Colt strapped to his hip. It was all that Ruff could do to keep his older brother from gunning down the ignorant cavalry officer.

"You *are* a fool," Ruff gritted at the captain when he'd calmed Houston down. "And if you should be lucky enough to survive this war, you'd better pray that you never come across me or any of my family."

Denton wanted to say something. His mouth worked but Ruff's eyes told him he wouldn't live long enough to finish even a single sentence, so the captain just clamped his mouth shut and spun away in a trembling rage.